"I'm supposed to be the cure for the town, *and* your cockatoo now?" Mary said as she ran her fingers along the row of CDs to find some new music for the bird.

That was a pretty lousy way to look at it. "I don't think of it like that," said Mac.

"That's how they put it. Something to bring everyone together. A big, splendid Christmas pageant to remind us of peace on earth, goodwill to men and such."

"I'm sorry you got hired to fix whatever it is people think I broke."

"I'm not sorry," she said, handing him a Mozart disc. "But if I get sorry, I'll make sure you're the first to know. I think it's sort of sweet, actually, how much people care about getting along here."

"If people cared about getting along here, you could have fooled me," Mac said. "There's a town hall meeting tomorrow night—come see how much getting along we actually do."

ALLIE PLEITER

Enthusiastic but slightly untidy mother of two, RITA® Award finalist Allie Pleiter writes both fiction and nonfiction. An avid knitter and nonreformed chocoholic, she spends her days writing books, drinking coffee and finding new ways to avoid housework. Allie grew up in Connecticut, holds a BS in Speech from Northwestern University and spent fifteen years in the field of professional fundraising. She lives with her husband, children and a Havanese dog named Bella in the suburbs of Chicago, Illinois.

Bluegrass Christmas
Allie Pleiter

Steeple
Hill®

Published by Steeple Hill Books™

STEEPLE HILL BOOKS

Steeple
Hill®

ISBN-13: 978-0-373-87556-6

BLUEGRASS CHRISTMAS

Copyright © 2009 by Alyse Stanko Pleiter

www.SteepleHill.com

Printed in U.S.A.

Better is one day in your courts
    than a thousand elsewhere;
    I would rather be a doorkeeper
    in the house of my God
    than dwell in the tents of the wicked.
              —*Psalms* 84:10

For Christina
For who she was, who she is,
and who she will be

Chapter One

While "Mac" MacCarthy hadn't counted on peace and quiet when he returned to his office, he hadn't anticipated an opera-singing cockatoo, either.

December might not go as well as he planned.

Assuming the only logical explanation, Mac pushed his way through the connecting interior doors of the bakery adjacent to his engineering office. "All right, Dinah, what did you do to him?"

Dinah Rollings, owner of the Taste and See Bakery, looked up from her cash register. "To whom?"

Mac cocked his head toward the racket behind him. "I've got Luciano Pavarotti in feathers perched on my credenza. Very funny. Now tell me what you did to Curly so I can hush him up before cats start prowling the alley."

With both doors open, Dinah could evidently hear the bird. Her face was half surprised, half amused. "Not bad. That's from *The Marriage of Figaro,* I think. Didn't peg you for an opera fan."

Mac looked quizzically at his smirking neighbor. "You didn't do this?"

She raised an eyebrow. "No."

"Gil?" Mac named his best friend who, while no fan of opera, had been known to love a good joke.

"Haven't seen him."

"Cameron?" Dinah's new husband didn't seem the type, but as a former New York City native, Cameron might have opera in his background. And pranks.

Dinah shot him an incredulous look. "Not a chance. Look, Mac, I don't know who might have…"

At that moment, Pavarotti—the *real* one—belted out the aria in question from the stairway between their businesses' doors. And Curly, Mac's yellow-crested-cockatoo-recently-turned-tenor, joined in.

The second-floor apartment had been empty since Cameron and Dinah got married. Evidently, it wasn't un-occupied anymore. Opera music flooded the hallway when Mac opened the door that led upstairs.

Dinah came to the door. "Okay, maybe I do know who could be…"

Curly chose that moment to chase his avian muse, leaving his perch in Mac's office to bolt up the stairway in a squawking white streak of feathers and falsetto.

Mac took the stairs three at a time, ruing the fact that repairmen at his house necessitated that Curly spend this week at the office with him. Curly almost never bolted, but when he did, he went full out. Nothing good could come from this. Mac was a few steps from the top when he heard the shriek.

Taking the last risers in two strides, Mac looked in the apartment door to find a blond woman cowering behind a music stand, holding what looked like a conductor's baton as if it were a broadsword. The operatic waltz blared from a set of speakers on either side of the room, and Curly stood ducking and bobbing in time with the music from atop a bookcase to Mac's right.

"What is that thing?" she said over the loud music. Actually, shouted might have been more accurate. Shouted with great annoyance. Curly wasn't a small bird, and he looked like an invading white tornado when he flew anywhere. Mac could only imagine how frightening, at first sight, it was.

"That's Curly," Mac introduced, feeling ridiculous as he yelled above the orchestration. "He won't hurt you. He seems to get a kick out of your music."

Her eyes were wide. "It's not mutual. Get him out of here." She seemed to realize how harsh she sounded, for a split second later she nervously inched over to the stereo and turned down the volume before adding "Please."

"Aww," Curly moaned as the music quieted down. That was pretty tame considering all the smart-aleck replies Mac had taught the bird over the years.

Dinah burst through the doorway behind Mac. "Mary! Are you okay?" She went over to her, while Mac called Curly down off the furniture. "I'm sure that's not the welcome you were expecting."

She had every right to be annoyed. Mac's own ma could get spooked by Curly on occasion, and she knew what to expect from the feathered comedian. Curly had the good sense to look sorry for his actions, putting his head down and trying to hide under Mac's arm. "I'm okay, I think," Mary said shakily. She was a pale thing, with ice-blue eyes and hair only a shade sunnier than Curly's snow-white coat. "No damage done, unless you count my nerves."

Dinah took her arm. "Mary…it's Thorpe, isn't it? Mary Thorpe, this great ferocious beast is Curly. And this is Mac

MacCarthy. Sorry you had to meet under such goofy circumstances."

"I'm really sorry about this. Curly's usually more civilized, and he's hardly ever in my office. And he's never gone bananas over…um…whatever you were playing… before. I didn't even know you were up here."

"It's okay," she allowed, but it didn't sound like she meant it.

"Curly," Dinah addressed the guilty bird, "you just scared the pants off Middleburg Community Church's new drama director."

Serves Mac right for skipping church to go to a special service with Gil and the guys from Homestretch Farm last Sunday. Gil ran a unique reform program on his horse ranch, and occasionally "the guys"—as the juvenile offenders were known around town—visited churches in their old neighborhoods. Still, Mary didn't look like the kind of person Mac thought would be leading drama at MCC. Actually, he didn't even know MCC was planning a dramatic performance. Since his decision to run for mayor against "lifetime incumbent" Howard Epson, hadn't Middleburg seen enough drama without having to make more? Not that anyone could be judged by how they weathered a cockatoo air strike, but this Mary seemed a little small and frail for the job. Mac had seen herds of mustangs more compliant than the MCC congregation. "Brave soul. Sorry you had Curly here for a welcoming committee."

At the mention of his name, Curly poked his head up and gave Mary a wolf whistle. Dinah laughed. Mac rolled his eyes and thought about getting a dog.

"Are you an opera buff?" Mary asked Curly, putting the baton thing down.

"Not until today," Mac replied. "I've never seen him do that before. He usually just bobs around when I play Bill Monroe."

Mary gave him a blank look.

"Bluegrass music. Curly's more used to that than…"

"Mozart?" she offered. She shrugged. "I give him points for good taste."

"And bad manners," Mac added as he nodded at the bird. "Say goodbye, you rascal."

"Bye bye," Curly squawked, winking one large black eye.

"I'm really sorry again. Welcome to Middleburg. I'll keep Curly under tight surveillance for the rest of the week until the repairmen are gone at my house." Mac shifted Curly to his left hand and extended his right.

She shook it. Her fingers were small but very strong. "I'll turn down the volume so he isn't tempted again."

Mac glared at Curly. "Tonight we bring your other cage over here. No more free flying around the office for you, bud—repairmen at home don't buy you a license to make trouble here for the neighbors."

"Happy Birthday, by the way," Dinah announced as they made their way downstairs. "Park your bird and come on over for some mint chocolate chip biscotti. You need them."

No one ever really *needed* anything from Taste and See, but Dinah was very good at making people think they did. The woman's trademark enthusiasm had only doubled since she had married Cameron Rollings, who used to live in the apartment Mary now occupied.

"My birthday's not for another twenty-nine days, Dinah."

"It's December first, so it's the first day of your birthday month. Close enough."

Mac furrowed his eyebrows. "You're not going to say that every day from now until the thirtieth, are you?"

"Whassamatta?" Dinah teased, reviving her native New Jersey accent. "The passing decade getting to you?"

Sure it was, but that's not the kind of question he was going to get into with armchair therapist-baker Dinah Rollings.

"No," he said, applying a smirk. "Turning thirty is not fatal. Not yet."

Mac had barely settled at his desk when he saw his mother press her face against the glass window of his front office. She yanked open the door and stood in the entryway, one hand on each hip, a look of utter disgust on her face.

"I can't take much more of this nonsense," she said as Mac's father filed in behind her. "Land sakes. If one more person looks at me sideways just because you up and ran for mayor…"

Mac stood up. His mama was in the room, after all. He had manners, even if his bird didn't. "I sort of thought all the ruckus would die down when the holidays got here."

Pa walked over to sit in the guest chair of Mac's office. "If you ask me, it's just gotten worse." He shook his head in a combination of disbelief and amusement. "Y'all know what you got into?"

"Yep."

He did. God had hounded him for months. He had very good, very personal reasons for taking this unconventional step. He was no stranger to wild ideas like this, anyway. As a matter of fact, Mac preferred to shun the norm whenever possible.

Which often drove his mama nuts.

Ma waved her hands in the air. "As if this campaign weren't enough. Now there's this Christmas pageant. I thought they were just off their rockers thinking that hiring some Christmas drama director would help mend fences. You know Howard's already announced that he's gonna be in the play, don't you? You'll have to as well, to keep Howard from getting the upper hand." She blew out a breath and shook her head. "This won't be a distraction, it'll be a disaster."

As far as Mac was concerned, it already was.

Mary Thorpe stood in the empty sanctuary of Middleburg Community Church and whispered a prayer of praise. *I'm here. Oh, Lord, it's amazing, what You've done. I'm here.* The place was just what she'd envisioned; a steepled white church with a blue door on a rolling hillside with an old organ and wooden pews that had seen decades of worship. It even had a preschool attached—something she loved. This afternoon, she'd heard a tiny-voiced rendition of "Jesus Loves Me" that made her heart bubble up in happy relief. This is it. A real Christmas.

She inhaled. The place was infused with a wholesome, old-fashioned atmosphere. She ran her hand across a chipped, aged music stand and thought of the soprano soloist catfight she'd witnessed at her previous part-time job as the second chair violinist at a Chicago opera company. Not to mention the near nuclear-level war between coworkers at her other temporary job at an advertising agency, and thought "no more." She picked up a battered hymnal from a nearby pew. From now it'll all be "Peace in the Valley." It's perfect.

"Are you ready?" Pastor Dave Anderson's voice broke

her reverie as he came up the aisle beside Mary. "Most folks were reluctant to do this drama at first, but Sandy Burnside, Howard and the other church elders convinced them." Anderson folded his arms across his chest and inclined his head toward Mary. "Still, y'all ought to be warned—they're an opinionated bunch, my feisty flock."

Mary tossed her blond ponytail over her shoulder and put her hands on her hips. "You haven't seen the Mid-American Orchestra String Section. *Opinionated* doesn't even begin to cover it. I'm ready to handle this."

"You know," the pastor amended, handing her a dozen copies of the nativity script they'd agreed upon, "I think maybe you are." He winked and crossed the sanctuary to his office.

Mary sat down on the pew and smoothed her hand over the stack of scripts. Middleburg was everything she'd prayed for. Her new address—Ballad Road—charmed her, dotted with shops and diners. And all the streets had musical names! Walking here, she had passed a quaint park with a sign that read "Tree Lighting, Wednesday, 7:00 p.m., Bake Sale to follow." Tree lighting. Bake sales.

God, in His wisdom, had led her to the middle of nowhere. The absolutely perfect place to disappear.

Chapter Two

This Sunday was just like his last Sunday at MCC; half the congregation avoided him in the church parlor after Sunday service. Dodging a sour look from Matt Lockwood, Mac focused his attention on Mary Thorpe. "Dinah told me you took cream and sugar," he explained, handing her a cup of coffee.

"She's nice. My apartment smells fabulous every morning, but I may put on ten pounds before New Year's." Mary smiled and waved to another member of the congregation. "They are an interesting bunch. Hey, I hear you're one of the reasons I'm here. Well, you and Howard Epson. The campaign and all. I thought I'd seen seriously dramatic local politics back in Chicago…."

Mac shrugged. "I'm not asking him to stop being mayor. I'm just asking to be a choice. We haven't had a choice for mayor since I was in high school. I think I'd do a great job, but if Howard wins, I'll actually be okay with it."

Mary took a sip of coffee and seemed to consider him.

Okay, it was sort of a cheesy speech, but that's really how he felt. He didn't want to start talking like a politician just because he ran for mayor, but lately stuff like that just jumped out of his mouth. "No really," he went on, not liking how she narrowed her eyes, "if people still want Howard, then that's what Middleburg should get. But they should *think* about whether they still want Howard."

"Speaking of what the people want, you do know you're both supposed to be in the production? Pastor Anderson told you, didn't he?"

"Oh, I've heard. I think I can manage something along the lines of third shepherd from the left."

She looked a bit tense. "Um, it's more involved than that. You've got a starring role. You're Joseph."

While Mac didn't like the idea of playing such a large role, he was sure Howard would be even less pleased. "And what about my worthy opponent?"

"Oh, we found the perfect part for him." She offered a weak smile. "He's God."

Mac stood in the barn at Homestretch Farm, having just finished a hearty Sunday dinner with Gil and his wife, Emily. After the meal, Gil had invited Mac to join him as he took care of a few things around the farm. That usually meant Gil had something on his mind, and Mac wasn't that surprised when Gil cleared his throat and sat down on a hay bale. "Emily said you got in another row with Howard at the diner."

Mac bristled. "You'd think I'd decided to do something life-threatening the way he and other folks talk. Everybody's always groaning about Howard, so why am I the first person willing to do something about it?" Mac had amazed even himself by how defensive he'd become on the subject. Running for Middleburg mayor did not qualify as a suicide mission. Still, when he announced his candidacy a few weeks back, people looked at him as if he'd just thrown himself on the end of a spear. They still did.

Gil fiddled with the large ring of keys he always carried. He had a habit of clanking them against his wedding ring. "You've showed me ads for four new cars in the last three months. New cars start catching your eye when you get antsy."

Mac rolled his eyes. "You've been reading Emily's magazines with all those quizzes or something. Wanting one new car does not constitute a midlife crisis. Pre-midlife crisis, rather," Mac corrected, as his grandfather was now in his late nineties and still remarkably sharp. He leaned back against a hay bale. "What are you getting at?"

"You like to stir up trouble, Mac. Always did. And a man with a weird bird and a fast sports car could just be scouting the next diversion." Gil looked serious.

"Meaning?" Mac knew lots of people who changed cars every two years.

"Are you running for mayor because it's what you want, or just because it'll get under everyone's skin?"

Mac was fully aware of his tendency toward shock value. He certainly could have thought he'd heard the Lord tell him to run for mayor when it might just be his appetite for ruffling feathers.

The truth was, actually, that Mac had been feeling restless. "Okay," he admitted to Gil, "I'm…how'd you put it? Antsy. But running for mayor isn't about that. I sat on this a long time. God's been after me for months, and yeah, I wasn't so sure it wasn't just me looking for a new thrill at first." It was something larger than that, something harder to explain. As Mac stared down the barrel of his thirtieth birthday, it felt as if life was sucking him into the expected routine. As if everyone else had figured out who he was supposed to be except him. He had no desire to "settle down" at the moment, but lots of folks—Ma chief among them—viewed him as simply staving off the inevitable. Predictability and inevitability chafed at Mac like he'd seen one of Gil's unbroken horses react to a bit in their mouths. If staying "unsettled" got under everyone's skin, they'd just have to get used to it.

"Only you," Gil said, "would think of running for mayor as 'a thrill.' Couldn't you just buy a horse or find a girl or something?"

Mac groaned.

"Relax, MacCarthy, I'm just pressing your buttons. I'm not out to trash your freewheeling, nonconformist lifestyle. Not that your mama hasn't asked me—repeatedly—to yak at you about the virtues of marriage. I just mostly want to know you're in the right place about this."

"That's just it. I'm not in the right place. I'm supposed to be someplace else."

Gil raised an eyebrow. Mac had been in Middleburg his whole life.

"Not *geographically*. Ever heard of a metaphor? I'm restless on the inside. Things don't feel comfortable any more. Or too comfortable, I don't know. I don't want to fade into the landscape here. Fall into some predictable rut. I really want this. I think I'm the guy, Gil. You know I've got a lot of ideas, and I think it's high time Middleburg even remembered they *had* a choice when it comes to a mayor."

"Sounds like a campaign slogan to me."

Mac was growing irritated by the fact that every time he voiced a well-phrased or complex idea, someone said "sounds like a campaign issue" or "that could be your campaign slogan." Middleburg's mayoral race wasn't large enough to even warrant a slogan. He didn't want to be the kind of guy whose civic agenda could fit on a bumper sticker.

"There are lots of ways to stand out in the world that doesn't cause so much trouble." Gil folded his arms across his chest. "You've hashed this out? Seriously?"

By "hashing something out," Gil meant praying over it. Seriously. Gil Sorrent took his job and his faith very seriously. It's what had made him able to withstand the tremendous pressures and setbacks of the criminal rehabilitation farm he ran. It's what made him the kind of man who didn't mince words and never let down his friends. "Yes," Mac replied, and he had. He'd felt like he'd wrestled forever with this decision to run. His ability to shake things up had led him down a few wrong turns over the years, and this seemed like a chance to finally channel that "talent" into something useful. To make his mark on the world before he slid into the bland predictability of… gasp…middle age. Shaking up was a far better choice than settling down, and this was a perfect opportunity to shake up for the good of Middleburg.

Gil took his answer at face value. Their friendship had lasted long enough to put sugarcoating or lying out of the question. "And you're sure?"

"Yes, I'm sure."

Gil sat back in the hay. "Well, you've actually got the personality to pull it off. Mostly. Emily'll burst out laughing the first time she has to say 'Your Honor'—I'm glad I don't have to." Emily and Gil had been on the city council before they'd married, and Gil had been the one to step down because spouses couldn't both remain in office.

"Maybe my first official duty will be to change that silly protocol." Mac gave his friend a nudge. "It might be worth it just to hear you say 'Your Honor' to me. Who knew I'd have to run for office to get any respect from you?"

Gil stretched a foot out in front of him. "I haven't said I'd vote for you yet. Howard's a bit hard to take sometimes, but he does a halfway decent job."

"You complain about Howard all the time. We spent half your time on the council fighting Howard."

"That's just it. When you're mayor, who will I have to complain to?"

"Maybe you won't have to complain at all. Have you considered that possibility?"

Gil grinned. "Not in the slightest."

Mary waved back at yet another person as she made her way up Ballad Road toward her apartment, half spooked and half amazed by how quickly she'd come to feel at home. So many people believed in God here. And not just the Sunday kind of belief. These were day-in, day-out believers. It was the perfect place for her to grow her shaky new faith.

Almost from the time she had committed her life to Christ, Chicago had begun to vex her. Her earlier jobs—however enviable—felt hollow and unsatisfying. Her own parents had trouble understanding how anyone could leave an orchestral position *and* freelance ad agency work to lead a Christmas drama, but it was just too hard to be a new Christian in her other world. That verse about "rather be a gatekeeper in the house of my God" kept running through her head. A fresh, humble start felt so much easier.

She stopped at the window of an adorable shop called West of Paris. A charming blue glass vase caught her eye. A housewarming gift for myself, she thought, picturing it with a few sprigs of holly on her tiny dining room table. She couldn't pull off a decorated tree this Christmas, even if her mom and dad came as planned, but the vase seemed just enough of a luxury to suit her mood. As she entered, a wave of wonderful scents and music-box Christmas carols washed over her.

"Merry Christmas," greeted the woman behind the counter. "I'm Emily Sorrent, we met at church. You're Mary, right?"

Mary was still adjusting to strangers calling her by name. "That's me."

"Must be hard to be in such a new place for the holidays. Away from home and family and all. Are you settling in okay?"

Mary imagined such a new start might be a challenge around Christmas—for other people. For her, it was the best present of all. "Just fine. It's so peaceful here."

Emily smiled. "Peaceful? Are you sure you're in Middleburg? I haven't seen our little town so worked up in years. No, Ma'am, 'peaceful' is not a word I'd use to describe Middleburg these days."

"That's okay. People used to think the big city orchestra where I worked was glamorous, but I wouldn't ever describe it that way, either."

Emily got a funny look on her face and turned away for a moment under the guise of arranging some holiday ornaments. Mary couldn't figure out what she'd said wrong. Maybe being new in town wasn't all fresh starts and clean slates. "I saw that blue vase in the window," she offered, changing the subject. "I think it would be perfect for my dining-room table."

"It's made by an artisan in Berea," Emily described, brightening. "That color is his trademark. Look, here's an

ornament he made in the same style." She held out a brilliant blue sphere with a sparkling gold center. "For your
tree."

"Oh," Mary interjected, brushing her off. "I don't think
I'll get a tree up this year."

Emily looked surprised. "No Christmas tree? You can't
be serious?"

Mary took in the store, and realized there must be six
fully decorated trees in Emily's shop alone. The woman
took her holiday decorating very seriously. Even for a
retailer.

"There's just me. I'd never be able to lug a tree up all
the stairs to my apartment, and I own about three ornaments, besides. Christmas was my busy season in past
years, and I never really had time to do all the trimmings.
I'll just take the vase, thanks."

Emily crossed her arms over her chest. "No, you
won't."

"What?"

"I don't know where you came from, but if you've
never had a real Christmas, Mary Thorpe, it's high time
you got one. And I am going to start you off. You can buy
the vase, but it just so happens I'm running a special today.
Every vase purchase comes with a free Christmas
ornament. And I happen to know a whole bunch of big
burly guys who will gladly lug your tree anywhere you
want it. MCC's new drama director will not be too busy
to have her own Christmas if I have anything to say about
it. And I'm on the church board and the town council, so
you can bet I have something to say about it."

Mary could only smile. "Okay, I'll think about it." She'd
just effectively been commanded to have a happy holiday,

and she couldn't be more pleased. She took the ornament and spun it in the sunlight, enjoying the blue and gold beams it cast around the room. "Dinah warned me about you."

Emily winked. "Oh, honey, you ain't seen nothing yet."

Chapter Three

Curly was singing.

This was a bit hard to take, especially because the bird insisted on singing the same piece of music he'd learned from Mary Thorpe's stereo earlier. Even an extra dose of sunflower seeds had failed to quiet the cockatoo. Mac looked up from the drafting table a third time, then let his forehead fall into his hand. "Enough, bird. You were funny once—and not really funny at that—but you're singing on my last nerve."

"Yep!" Curly squawked, and Mac regretted—for the umpteenth time today—teaching the bird to agree with everything he said.

There was only one thing for it. Maybe the sheer repetition of the aria had stomped out his neurons, but Mac was relatively certain the only way to stop this bird from singing the same thing over and over was to give him something new to sing. And while the Kentucky Fight Song might have been a masculine choice, Mac also knew that would wear even worse than the opera.

He felt like a complete idiot walking up the stairs to

Mary Thorpe's apartment with Curly doing the bird equivalent of humming—a sort of half whistling noise accompanied by a comical head bob—on his shoulder. He didn't, however, have Mary's phone number, and he was sure in another hour he'd be incapable of putting a sentence together. "Behave yourself for both our sakes," he told Curly as he knocked on the door.

She opened the door cautiously, trying not to broadcast her alarm at seeing Curly. "Hi there," she said too kindly, forcing her smile.

"Do you think," Mac spoke, finding the words more idiotic by the second, "we could teach Curly something else? I'm living with a broken record here and it's driving me nuts." On a whim he looked at the bird and stated, "You need a bigger repertoire, don't you, boy?"

"Yep!" Curly squawked, nodding.

"No offense to your opera," Mac confessed, "but I don't think I could take even my favorite song nonstop like he's been doing."

She opened the door a bit more. He could see she'd gotten much farther in her unpacking, and the small apartment was starting to look like a home. "Haven't you taught…" she inclined her head toward the feathered occupant of Mac's right shoulder.

"Curly."

"Curly any other songs?"

Curly bobbed a bit at the mention of his name. "No, actually. I didn't know he could sing until you moved in. Seems bluegrass doesn't interest him, but whatever it was…"

"Mozart," she reminded, a hint of a smile finally making its way across her features.

"…catches his fancy. So," Mac continued, daring to

bring Curly off his shoulder to sit on his forearm, "you got any more Mozart for Curly to learn? A CD of something quiet and background-ish to get me through these last two days?"

Mary opened the door wide, raising one eyebrow. "Mozart didn't write elevator music."

"There's got to be something. As long as it's not the 1812 Overture, it'll be an improvement."

"I'm not in the habit of giving singing lessons. Not even to humans."

Curly started in on the aria again.

"I'll pay you. Another ten minutes of this and you can name your price."

Mary looked at the bird. "Hush up, Curly." She had a teacher's voice—gentle, but you knew she meant business.

Wonder of wonders, Curly hushed. *Now* Curly gets co-operative? Where was all that avian obedience ten minutes ago? "Whoa," Mac reflected, turning Curly so he could look him in one traitorous black eye. "Teach me *that* first."

Mary shrugged, as if she didn't have an answer to that, and motioned Mac and Curly into her apartment. Mac was right—she had settled in. The place looked more lived-in than the months Cameron Rollings had laughingly called it his "bachelor pad." She went to her bookcases, traveling through her CD collection with dainty flicks of her finger. "I'm thinking he needs voices, so none of the chamber music will do—that's all mostly instrumental. Oh," she noted and plucked a CD from the shelf, "this might work."

She inserted the disc into her player and a soft, high, female voice lilted out of the speakers. Curly cocked his head to one side. Mary looked at Curly and sang along, conducting with her forefinger. Curly began inspecting Mac's watch.

"I'm thinking that's a 'no.'"

Mary pulled another selection and popped it into her sound system.

The same tenor voice as Curly's previous obsession came over the speakers, but this time Pavarotti was singing Italian songs. The kind guys in striped shirts sang as they pushed boats through Venice. Not very hip, but still better than opera. Mary walked up to Curly and began singing along, conducting with her fingers again. This time Curly took notice, swooping his head around to match the movement of her hand. She caught Mac's eye, and they both nodded. "I suppose technically I have you to thank for my job, since part of my job description is to take everyone's mind off the mayoral conflict. This lesson will be on the house." She sang a few more bars as the chorus came around again, and Curly began making noises. "Future lessons from the tonic for Middleburg's mayoral malaise might cost you."

"Very catchy, but I don't think it's the civic disaster they're making it out to be."

"For what it's worth," Mary said over the swelling music, "neither do I."

"There will be no more lessons. The floor guys will be done with my house by Friday. After that, Mr. Music here stays home." Pavarotti launched into another song, a Dean Martin number Mac recognized from his ma's record collection. "Who knew my bird has such questionable taste in music?"

"Curly has very good taste, actually."

When she looked at him, he realized he'd just insulted her CD collection. Just hitting them out of the ballpark here, MacCarthy, aren't we? She didn't say so, but it glared out of her eyes just the same; better taste than you, evidently.

"Could I make a copy of that CD?" he said sheepishly.

"Music is copyrighted material, Mr. MacCarthy. I'm sure you wouldn't take kindly to my Xeroxing your latest blueprints and passing them around, would you?"

"Okay," Mac conceded slowly, feeling like this conversation had started off badly and was slipping further downhill fast.

She softened her tone as she handed him the CD. "But you may borrow this one for the moment. If Curly needs further…inspiration…I'm sure you can find your way to a copy. An original copy, bought and paid for."

"Absolutely. You got it." Mac took the slim plastic box from her, and Curly put his head up to it, rubbing against the corner in a disturbingly lovesick gesture. "And, well, I'm sorry you got hired to fix whatever it is people think I broke."

"I'm not sorry," she commented, opening the door for them to go, "but if I get sorry, I'll make sure you're the first to know. I think it's sort of sweet, actually, how much people care about getting along here."

"If people cared about getting along here, you could have fooled me," Mac observed. "There's a town hall meeting tomorrow night—come see how much *getting along* we actually do."

"Pastor Anderson," Mary began.

"Dave," the older man corrected.

"Dave," she said, still not entirely comfortable with the concept of calling a member of the clergy by his first name. Up until this summer, she'd seen people like Dave Anderson as almost a different species. High, lofty souls who didn't bother with the likes of "sinners" like herself. Not that she thought of herself as a sinner. She was pretty proud of all her accomplishments then. Back before she'd realized "achievement" didn't always translate into "happiness."

It was, in fact, happiness she was speaking of—at least to Dave. "You know, Dave," she continued carefully, "I'm worried about how much people are expecting out of this Christmas drama."

He smiled. "You'll do fine. Actually, when you think about it, you can't help but do fine. You're our first drama coordinator, so folks don't have anyone to compare you to. You can't help but improve us. And they like you already—I can tell."

How to say this? "It's not the drama I'm worried about. It's the...well, the result you're looking for. Don't you think town unity's kind of a high expectation for a little church drama?"

Pastor Dave sat back in his chair. "That's because you're expecting it to be a little church drama. It will be church, it will be drama, but I guarantee it won't be little. Complications might be just what the doctor ordered in this case." His eyebrows lowered in concern. "I want you to pour your creative energies into making this as all-consuming as possible."

"Aren't there more direct ways to resolve the town's conflict?"

"I suppose there would be—if the town was willing to admit they *had* a conflict. Most of them want a big Christmas extravaganza to make them feel good. Just you and I and a few other wise folk realize they need something to agree on to take their minds off the many disagreements."

"What about Mac and Howard?"

The pastor chuckled. "I think Mac knows he stirred up a hornet's nest. He enjoys it—always has been one to whip things up a bit. I think Howard feels the conflict, but he's likely to read it all wrong. He feels attacked because I think he'd much rather change on his own terms, not on those of someone like Mac."

"But Howard was bound to retire someday." Mary leaned one elbow on the corner of Dave's desk. She was still sorting out the complexities of "simple little Middleburg."

"I'm not so sure Howard's caught on to that truth yet. He's been mayor for so long he may not remember how to be anything else. We've got sixth-graders who've never known Howard as anything but mayor. You have to respect that."

"All things considered, I'm not so sure a Christmas pageant is the way to cope. We're sticking a tiny bandage on a great big wound here."

"Miss Thorpe, you ever been a parent?" He got up from his chair and walked over to his office windows overlooking the preschool. "Ever given a toddler a bandage?"

"I'm sure I have at some point." Mary didn't really see where he was heading.

"They *believe* it makes things better. A child may get stitches for a nasty gash, but they won't calm down until somebody puts on a bandage. It's the stitches that do the real healing, but they still need the bandage. You and I know it's an illusion, but that doesn't mean it doesn't work." He grinned and pointed at her. "Some of my best work is done with Band-Aids."

Mary blinked. "I'm a diversionary tactic?"

He walked toward her. "Would it make it easier if I said you were a coping mechanism?"

This had started out as a simple job. A calmer life serving an undiluted purpose, a chance for Mary to get away from the agenda-laden world of professional music and

advertising. Suddenly she had more agendas than a dip-
lomat and a goal so complex and obscure she could no
longer say what it truly was. "I've got a headache just trying to make sense of this." She looked up at him. "Can I
have a Band-Aid?" It was supposed to be a joke, but Mary
couldn't quite muster the confidence to pull it off.

"Take two rehearsals and call me in the morning,"
Pastor Dave joked.

Mary sat in her living room that afternoon, trying to
make sense of it all. How many people thought of the
drama as just a nice holiday event? How many of them
were aware of its secondary goal of unifying the community? How to balance the two? *Lord, I prayed for hours over
this job. I asked You to take me someplace where I could
figure out all this faith stuff. Someplace easier than
Chicago. This isn't looking easier.*

Mary smiled as the faint strains of Pavarotti's tenor
voice singing "Ave Maria" reached her ears. She wondered
if Mac found it an improvement over the Mozart aria. It
was hard to think of that bird crooning a ballad. Too bad
it wasn't summertime; she'd have been able to hear Curly
through the open window.

Then again, maybe it was better all the windows were
shut. She wasn't entirely sure Curly the cockatoo was up
to the high note at the end of the song.

Laughing at the thought of the bird straining to hit the
note, his creamy neck extended and his feathers fluttering,
Mary reached for the mail that had been forwarded from
her old Chicago apartment. She sorted through the en-
velopes until she spotted the familiar gray stationery of
Maxwell Advertising. She'd forgotten, until now, that she
had one more bonus coming. She opened the envelope and

slid out a substantial check. How ironic that her "swan song" had been her most lucrative project ever. God had given her enough resources to take whatever job she wanted, wherever she wanted. And He had brought her here. Maybe, for now, she could trust that, despite the growing complexities.

Mac shut the door to his office with a fierce *thunk* and walked briskly toward Deacon's Grill. A piece of pie couldn't really do anything about the storm of aggravation he carried around, but it couldn't hurt, either. At least a warm cup of coffee might soothe his annoyance. "Peace on earth, goodwill toward men?" Today felt more like "profits on earth, bad will toward any consumer." No wonder Ma had asked him to handle the procurement of one of those idiotic Bippo Bears for his nephew, Robby. Finding the fuzzy blue singing bear proved to be more like warfare than Christmas shopping. Not counting the two trips to two separate malls yesterday, Mac had just spent three hours on the phone and Internet in search of a Bippo Bear. He sat down on his counter stool at the Grill with such force that the thing rocked under his weight.

Gina, no stranger to diner psychology, read his body language and immediately swapped out the ordinary sized stoneware mug at the island for a much larger one she produced from under the counter. Gina was smart. "Regulars" who obviously had a bad day were quickly given what she called a "comfort cup." That was Gina's entirely-too-female term for "the really big mug of coffee." He accepted it gladly, needing the hot beverage too much to care that it announced his disgruntled mood to the rest of the diner. He was pretty sure his entrance had already done that, anyway.

"And a Merry Christmas to you, too, sugar," Gina said as she slid the sugar container in front of Mac withholding the cream pitcher. Apart from baking the best pies around, Gina also had a great memory for customer preferences. "Rough going on the campaign trail?"

Campaign? Who had time for a campaign when Christmas shopping was sucking half his day into the trash can?

Gina's reference to the mayoral campaign halted Howard Epson in his conversation. Mac hadn't even noticed Howard as he came in, he was so annoyed. Epson and his wife were sitting in their favorite corner booth with Mary Thorpe of all people, probably advising her on the mayor's expected role in all holiday ceremonies. Divine drama aside, he was sure Howard took pains to stay a highly visible mayor during the MCC's Christmas season.

Mac swallowed a gulp of coffee, telling himself to back down off his soapbox. Howard could get to him so easily these days. They'd chalked up a lot of reasons to dislike each other over the years, some of which everyone knew—Mac had a long, checkered history of behavior Howard disapproved of—and some that were more private.

Years ago, when Mac was a senior in high school, he'd pulled a prank of sorts that ended up with Howard in the crosshairs. Actually, to call it a prank was making it too deliberate—it was more of an impulsive reaction. A stupid, angry gesture that ended up damaging church property and Howard's car one night. The whole town had seen the wreckage, but no one had ever discovered Mac was behind it. When God and the passing years finally granted Mac some maturity, he'd still never found it in himself to fess up to the deed. Howard would surely blow it way out of proportion, and Mac had convinced himself it was one of those secrets best left buried. Not that it hadn`t nagged at him over time, but lots of stuff about Howard bothered Mac—civic and personal. It was one of the reasons he felt God had asked him to run for mayor; to prove he was better than the angry kid he once was.

Mac caught sight of one of Howard's campaign brochures on the place setting next to Mary. She was surely getting a suggestion or two about the proper way to vote. At Gina's mention of the campaign, Howard inclined his balding head slightly toward Mac and stopped his words midsentence. Even the French fry on the way to his mouth had been stilled halfway. Mary Thorpe caught Mac's glance for a split second before looking down into her pie.

"No," Mac answered Gina's earlier question clearly enough for Howard to hear. "The campaign's going *fine*." He tried not to emphasize the word too much. "As a matter of fact, it's a pathetic stuffed animal that has me riled up. I've just wasted half the morning trying to find something called a Bippo Bear for my nephew. Evidently even the secret service couldn't get their hands on one of these if they wanted to—and don't you know, it's the one and only thing Robby wants for Christmas."

"A what?" Gina asked, flipping open her order pad and pulling a pen out of from behind her ear.

"A Bippo Bear. It's blue and sings to you and can't be found for love or money. Already. And it's still early December. What is it with these toy people? Don't they realize they have to make enough of these things to go around? Do they enjoy disappointing kids and making parents crazy?"

Drew Downing looked up from his sandwich a few seats to Mac's left. "Bippo Bear? I saw something on the news last night about those." Drew used to host a church renovation television show until an episode had brought him to Middleburg and introduced him to the love of his life, hardware store owner Janet Bishop. The man knew a thing or two about the power of advertising. "I saw one go for a hundred dollars yesterday on an Internet auction site. This year's must-have toy, it seems."

"Why does there have to be a 'must-have' toy, anyway?" Mac complained in a cranky voice. "My nephew doesn't even like stuffed animals. I'll spend two weeks tracking down one of those things and he'll play with it for two hours before he tires of it."

"Oh, yeah," remembered Gina, "it's that commercial that's on eleven hundred times a day. How could I forget?" She began to hum a few bars of the annoying little Bippo Bear song.

The one Mac had been forced to listen to for forty minutes while on hold with the toy company in a misguided attempt to locate a Canadian retailer. While he thought going foreign to be a smart alternative, the cheerful customer service representative at the Bakley Toy Factory informed him that he was her sixtieth such call of the day.

"Mary," came Howard's voice over his angry thoughts, "are you all right? Your pie okay? You look like you swallowed your fork all of a sudden."

Mac glanced over and Gina raised her head from her order pad. Middleburg's newest resident did indeed appear a bit ill, but Mac doubted it was anything Gina fed her. Howard had probably just said something insensitive, as he was known to do when he became overly focused on impressing someone new.

"Oh, no," Mary protested loudly. "It's wonderful pie." Mac recognized the forced cheerfulness she'd used when telling him it was "okay" that a maniac bird attacked her in her living room.

"Hi, Mary." Mac waved and she waved back, but it was a weak, wobbly gesture. "Hello, Howard," Mac said more formally.

Howard had become extremely formal with Mac since he'd announced his candidacy. "Good afternoon, Mac-Carthy." Howard had begun calling him Mr. MacCarthy or just MacCarthy whenever they met now. He didn't even turn around, just twisted his head half a turn in Mac's direction and puffed up as though they were on podiums debating issues instead of just eating in the same diner.

"Apple as usual, Mac?" Gina interjected. Her tone of voice seemed to imply that all conflicts could easily be solved with the right slice of pie. "I'll even heat it up for you, how's that?"

"Perfect." He settled more peaceably onto his stool and inhaled the rich aroma rising out of his wonderfully enormous coffee mug. "I refuse to let a stuffed blue bear steal my holiday."

"Good plan," Drew Downing offered. "But I know what you mean. My sister e-mailed me yesterday, and she wasn't too subtle about asking me what strings I could pull to get my hands on one of those for her daughter. The old 'Can't you do this 'cause you're famous?' ploy."

Mac smiled. While Drew still made occasional appearances for his former *Missionnovation* television show, Mac had taken to ribbing him about his "has been" status. And really, Downing had just walked head-on into another teasing with that remark. "You're just not famous enough anymore, sport," he taunted, digging into the pie Gina had just placed in front of him.

Drew caught onto the game and cracked a wide grin. "Hey, I still rate. I still have fans. My Web site got six hits last week."

"Wow. Maybe I should ask you to endorse my candidacy." Mac thought he'd said it quietly enough to escape Howard's hearing, but the man seemed to have radar for that sort of thing, and Mac saw his head incline slightly in his direction again.

Drew caught the exchange. "I've stayed a star as long as I have because I know which battles *not* to get into."

"You're a Middleburg resident now, you'll have to vote soon enough."

"A gratefully private matter, Mr. MacCarthy." Drew poured more cream into his own coffee. "God bless democracy."

Mac leaned in on one elbow. "Why do I get the feeling if Howard wins, you'll tell him you voted for him, but if I win you'll say I had your vote?"

Howard wasn't even pretending not to listen now. He'd turned halfway around to face Mac and Drew, his attention openly on the conversation.

"Eat your pie, gentlemen," Gina cut in, brandishing the pie-cutter knife she was holding. She tilted the spatula in Howard's direction. "All of you."

Drew straightened in his chair. "Don't anger the pie lady," he declared as if he and Mac had been caught passing notes in class.

"Good policy," Mac whispered back loudly, glad to have enough humor to still make a joke. Honestly, his short fuse was way too short lately. He needed to remember to get out more. The combination of year-end workload and campaign tasks on top of his new commission as Bippo Bear procurement agent had gotten to him fast. *I'm going to need an easy nature and a mile-long fuse to be mayor,* he told himself. *That's a tall order for the likes of me. Are You listening, Lord?*

Chapter Four

It couldn't be. I mean, yes, it was Kentucky, and it wasn't like they didn't have snakes in Illinois, but they didn't take up residence under the kitchen sink. That was the beauty of living five stories up in a city. The wildlife stayed *in the wild*. Mary stood very still, both hands vise-locked onto the broomstick she now pushed against the cabinet door. Nothing, no one could get her to stop holding that cabinet door shut and keeping that lethal creature inside. Mary heard something shuffle behind the door and swallowed a scream.

Think. You're a smart girl, think.

No coherent thought came to mind.

If she screamed, surely someone in the building would hear her. Did birds have good hearing? Would Curly be able to hear her even if Dinah or Mac couldn't? The scene of Curly getting Mac's attention, *"Lassie, what do you mean Timmy's stuck down the well?"*-style, flashed absurdly through her head. Town newcomer saved by vigilant cockatoo. It'd be out over the Internet in seconds, along with a photo of herself being loaded, pale and shaking, into a

Woodford County ambulance. Sunflower seed reward for snake-killing bird.

Not helpful, Mary. Think. Think rationally.

I can't think rationally, there's a python under my sink.

You don't even know if it's venomous. There are perfectly harmless snakes, her rational side argued.

It will eat you in one gulp, her terrified side rebutted, very successfully.

"Mac!" she yelled, trying for some ridiculous reason to sound calm. When no reply came, she tried "Dinah!" After half a minute and another sinister sub-sink shuffle, Mary cried, "Curly!"

Nothing.

Well of course he can't hear you, it's winter and the windows are shut. A building as old as this must have thick walls. *Lord Jesus! I haven't even had a year as a Christian, I can't be ready for Heaven yet! Save me!*

The floor. She could use the floor. Forcing in a deep breath, Mary tried to mentally compare the floor plan of her apartment with Mac's office below. She'd only seen it once, but it was enough to be reasonably sure that his office was directly below where she was standing. If she just thumped, it would only sound like she was moving things. It had to sound deliberate. Somewhere, out of the dark trivia-hoarding recesses of her brain, Mary retrieved the Morse code for SOS. Three short beeps, followed by three long beeps, followed by three short ones again. While the concept of long beeps didn't directly translate into foot-stomping, Mary guessed she could come close enough. If that didn't work, she could still reach the toaster and begin throwing it on the ground until Mac was convinced the walls were caving in up here.

Tap-tap-tap. STOMP. STOMP. STOMP. Tap-tap-tap.

Mary dug her heel into the floor to produce the loudest possible staccato taps. *Lord Jesus, please let Mac know Morse code and not let him think I'm an amateur flamenco dancer.* She repeated the sequence again.

Curly noticed first. Mac looked up from his papers, only barely noticing an unusual noise. Mary sure was doing a lot of banging around up there. Rhythmic, too. Exercise?

Tap-tap-tap. BANG-BANG-BANG. Tap-tap-tap. Curly came down off his perch in the window to stand on Mac's desk lamp. "Your new friend is a bit odd," Mac remarked, raising his eyes to the ceiling. "Even for city folk."

The succession of noises repeated again, louder. Folk dancing? Some jumpy new Chicago fitness fad? Morse code? Mac reached for his calculator, chuckling.

Until the bangs repeated.

Morse code? He knew Morse code. He knew the signal she was banging out, or knew it once. Mac stared at Curly, trying to pull the information out of the back recesses of his memory until…

Tap-tap-tap. BANG-BANG-BANG. Tap-tap-tap. SOS. That was Morse code for SOS.

No way. That was absurd.

The series of bangs came faster and louder now. Quite clearly three short taps followed by three more big bangs followed by three more short taps. SOS. Or something too close to it to ignore. But really, how many people knew Morse code, much less stomped it on their floors? Still, he'd never forgive himself if something really had been wrong and he'd dismissed it. Dashing up there would make him look like a complete idiot—if she was fine. "You think?" Mac said to Curly, pushing back his desk chair.

Curly was already flying toward the door. "Yep!"

* * *

He stood at the door, hands poised to knock, and listened for another set of stomps. He'd almost talked himself out of knocking, sure she would find his visit an example of overdone small-town meddling, when he heard the moan. It was not, by any stretch of the imagination, a calm sound. At that point, knocking was no longer needed. Mac flung Curly off his forearm and twisted Mary's door handle, pushing the door wide open and sprinting inside.

"Oh, Lord Jesus, save me from that thing! Who's there?"

Mac followed her voice into the kitchen to find Mary Thorpe impaling her cabinet with a broomstick. Throwing all her slight weight against that door as if an 800-pound gorilla were hiding under her sink. It was comic—in an alarming kind of way—until whatever it was behind there made a considerable racket. Then it wasn't so funny.

Mary shifted her weight, pressing harder against the broom handle, and squeaked "Mac! It's in there!"

"*What's* in there?" Mac said as calmly as he could while scanning her kitchen for heavy objects. He strode to her and took the broomstick, keeping pressure against the door.

She bolted away from him the minute he had a grip, backing into a corner on the other side of the kitchen, her chest heaving. "I don't know. I only heard it. I sure wasn't going to open the door and introduce myself."

Mac worked himself closer to the cabinet, hand-over-hand down the broom handle until he held the door shut with his boot. Nothing pushed back against him, but things were definitely moving around in there. A constant, steady rustle rather than an irregular scurrying. Mary Thorpe had a snake in her kitchen. Not exactly the warmest of Kentucky welcomes. "It sounds like you've got a snake in there," he confirmed, trying to keep his tone conversational, as if kitchen snake visits were commonplace. They weren't rare, but it was unusual to get one on the second floor in December.

"Ooo," she winced, hunching up her shoulders and squinting her eyes shut. "I knew it. Snakes. I hate snakes. I mean I really hate snakes."

Mac started searching for something forklike to trap the head. Somehow he didn't think Mary Thorpe would take kindly to having her carving fork used to skewer a snake. "It's probably a harmless milk snake. They like buildings."

"*Probably* harmless?" Unconvinced didn't do her tone of voice justice.

"There just aren't that many that can hurt you around here. Be thankful it's not a skunk in there." Mac looked at the cabinet again. Don't let it be a skunk in there. "Is your phone hooked up?"

"Yes."

"Is it cordless?"

"Uh-huh." Her shoulders softened the smallest amount.

He looked her straight in the eye, giving her his best *remain calm, things are under control* voice. "Okay, here's what we're going to do. Go get your phone, and we'll call Janet at the hardware store to bring over a snake catcher. She's thirty seconds away, so we'll have whatever it is out of your kitchen in ten minutes flat."

Mary nodded.

"So now you need to go get the phone."

That snapped her out of her shock. She came back with the phone and a roll of duct tape. When he raised his eyebrow at the second item, she explained "Maybe we can seal him in there until Jane gets here."

Mac allowed himself a small chuckle. "It's *Janet,* and I don't think the duct tape will be necessary." He gave her the phone number, and she put the handset in speaker mode while she dialed.

"Bishop Hardware."

"Hey there, Vern, it's Mac. Is Janet around?" he conversed in a friendly voice. Vern would have a field day with a situation like this, especially given his flair for the dramatic. He'd probably play it up, making Mary think a Komodo dragon was gnawing away the woodwork under her sink, hatching little ones who would feast on Mary in her sleep. No, this was definitely a situation that called for Janet's calm female touch. His call was right on the money, and Janet promised to be there within three minutes with the necessary equipment.

"Got a flashlight?" Mac asked, thinking Mary needed a bit of distraction while they waited.

"Um…I think so." Her voice was still a good octave higher than normal. "Why?" she inquired from the other room.

He thought that was obvious. "We need to see who we're dealing with here."

She shot back into the room, flashlight in hand. "Don't you open that door." Just then she noticed Curly perched on the back of her kitchen chair—she'd been oblivious to his presence until then. "Hi, Curly." She said it calmly, as if Curly's intruder status had been stripped—he was a friend now compared to the new invader in her home.

"Hello," Curly responded amiably.

"Mary," Mac began, "we can't get him out without opening the door. It could just be a tiny little mouse making all that noise." He didn't really think that, but it sounded better than "It will go more smoothly if I can see how many feet long the big nasty snake is before we kill it." Said villainous creature chose that moment to push a little against the cabinet door, making Mac gulp and Mary shriek.

"Don't you dare open that door."

"Okay, the door stays shut until Janet gets here. No peeking." After a tense moment, he added, "You know, you could just take Curly down to the bakery and both get a cracker or something while we take care of your little guest here." Mac doubted the vision of a snake twitching on the end of a stick would do much for her nerves, even if he was transporting the harmless creature downstairs to release him outside unharmed as Janet would insist he do.

"I'm staying," she countered, the bravado in her voice was a good, if unconvincing, attempt. "But *over here.*" She kept the kitchen table between herself and the sink.

"You know Morse code?" Mac noted, hitting on a diversionary topic while the door thumped against his shin again. Okay, maybe it was a slightly large animal in there.

"Just the important words," she indicated, staring directly at the cabinet door. "You know, yes, no, help, SOS, pizza.'"

"Pizza?"

"Sergeant Sam's gave you four dollars off your pizza if you ordered in Morse code. College."

Mac laughed. She didn't look like the kind to inhale pizza—definitely more the Brie-and-salad type. "And they say our educational system is in crisis."

"Well, before today, I thought that was a piece of useless trivia."

"Hello?" came Janet's voice from the still-open front door of Mary's apartment. "Animal rescue here!"

Mac bought Mary a second cup of coffee as they sat at the little table in Dinah's bakery. "The snake wasn't *that* big."

Mary shot him a look. "*Any* snake is too big in my book. Any snake in my kitchen, that is. I'm not against them in general. God's creatures and all. I'm sure they serve a very important link in the food chain. Just as long as that food chain stays out of my apartment."

Mac hoisted his coffee and swallowed a laugh. "You were very brave. Even Janet was twitching a bit when we finally got that thing out of there—he was a feisty one. But totally harmless. Really. He posed more danger to Curly than to you or me."

She doubted that. All snakes had teeth, venomous or not. She wasn't in any hurry to add "snakebite" to her list of thrilling new experiences. "How is Curly, by the way?" she asked as she changed the subject to a different species. "Expanding his playlist?"

Mac made a face. This was obviously not an improvement in topics. "Not by a long shot." He ran a hand through his head full of unruly sandy-colored hair. "He likes whatever it is you gave him—I have a copy on order, by the way, so you can have yours back soon—and I suppose that means he may take up something from it one of these days, but…"

"But…" she prompted as if she didn't know what was coming.

His bottle-green eyes took on a teasing expression. "Let's just say the Three Tenors haven't made it to a quartet."

"Still drowning in *The Marriage of Figaro?*" Mary laughed at the thought of that odd bird's fascination with operatic tenors. "Maybe we can teach him a Christmas carol and put him in the play."

"Only if you include one of Howard's horses, too. He'll want equal time."

Mary put down her cup. "Have you always been a thorn in Howard's side?"

Mac sat back in the chair. He wasn't an enormous man, more of a strong, lean build, but he looked too big for the bakery's delicate chairs. He legs refused to fit under the small round table. He flexed his fingers, putting his answer together in his head. Mac's broad, tawny hands looked as though they divided their time between paperwork and oil changes. The kind of man who could tinker with a spreadsheet just as easily as he could an engine. Evidently she'd asked a delicate question.

"'Spose I have. We go back a bit, you could say. And yeah, Howard and I clash on a regular basis. We see things differently. But I'm not out to get him, if that's what you're asking."

"Does he think you are? Out to get him, I mean?"

Mac kicked his legs out, and Mary felt like they extended into the center of the room. The man took up space—literally and figuratively—and he was comfortable with it. "I quit trying to figure out what Howard's thinking a long time ago. Still, I reckon Howard would've gotten his dander up at *anyone* who took him on, even if it wasn't someone like me. That's one of the reasons I felt I ought to be the one to run. That kind of heat don't bother me much."

That kind of heat. Meaning all that attention. Mary had learned a while back that men who liked attention didn't much care if it was positive or negative attention. Her former boss, Thornton Maxwell, didn't care if the business columns praised him or bashed him, as long as they discussed him. What was that old saying? "All press is good press." Still, Mary wasn't sure it was right to paint all extroverts with the same sinister brush as Thornton. Just because a guy took the lead didn't mean he was ready to squash everyone in his path. And it needed saying that not one of Mary's artsy advertising colleagues or cerebral music composition classmates could have dispatched that snake so calmly. Mac looked like an alligator would have posed an amusing challenge, or maybe some antlered forest beast would have ended up mounted to the hood of his truck.

If he owned one. Mary had never seen him drive anything but the shiny orange sports car that pulled into the spot in front of MacCarthy Engineering every morning. She still couldn't quite see how that tall man folded into that zippy little car.

"So why'd you do it?" Mary prodded.

"Run?"

"Yeah. Why not just wait until he retired?"

"Howard? Retire? Doubt he would. Not that you shouldn't like your job, but Howard loves his a bit too much. I'm not even sure he consciously knows he projects the 'mayor for life' thing, but I don't think he can see himself *not* in charge. He doesn't know how to follow. The man's in charge of stuff he's not even in charge of." Mac finished off his coffee and pointed at her. "And you ought to keep that in mind. Your newcomer status may be the only thing keeping him from taking over the Christmas drama. And he still might. I saw him in the diner earlier—he's just warming up on you. I give it two weeks before you're knee-deep in Howard."

Mary raised an eyebrow. Mac wasn't looking humble himself at the moment, either. "'Knee-deep in Howard'?"

"Okay, that sounded a bit ridiculous. But you know what I mean."

She shot him a look.

"For what it's worth, I don't think Howard's all bad. His motives are good. He believes he's got the town's best interests at heart." Mac wiped his hands down his face, as if he still hadn't found the words to explain what he was trying to say. "I love it here, but I get so annoyed with people for being so…predictable. People here fall into life by default. No one's run against Howard because everybody is so used to Howard as mayor. But Howard's so stuck in how everything's always been that he can't see the possibilities. I don't want Middleburg to die off just because it's the path of least resistance. Life should never be the path of least resistance, the expected thing."

"And you're the new possibility?" She hoped her skepticism for his speech didn't show.

"Sounds corny, doesn't it? But, well, yeah. I prayed about it for weeks when I first got the idea. Even *I* don't tilt the world sideways without thinking it through. But the honest truth is that I believe this is what God wants me to do. Run, at least. I'll leave the part about whether or not I win up to Him."

She'd seen him at church, heard him lead prayers during services, but it was different to hear him talking about how God affected his everyday life. She was just getting used to this praying-over-decisions thing. Part of it was wonderful; she could bring the Lord of the universe in on even her smallest decisions. Another part of it was frightening, because she'd given up having the final say. God hadn't said no to anything she'd asked Him yet, and she wasn't sure how she'd handle it when He did.

She looked at Mac again. Most of the people she knew in Chicago had so many layers, so many overlapping hidden agendas that a simple conversation gave her a headache. Mac was just the opposite—living, walking "what you see is what you get." It was as unsettling as it was refreshing.

Chapter Five

"I memorized a line today," Gil bragged to Mac as they brought more wood in from the pile in Mac's backyard. He puffed up and bellowed, "Spare not one!" into the night air. Mac had to agree with the casting; Herod was a very good use of Gil's commanding baritone.

"I'm shaking in my boots, your majesty. And you have all of what, six lines?"

"Seven."

"Ain't that useful. I, on the other hand, have no less than forty-two lines to occupy my whopping load of free time."

"Star." It wasn't a compliment.

"I got 'em typed out onto index cards and stacked up on my dashboard. I go over them at stop lights and while I'm waiting at the train crossing. Because *that's* how much free time I have."

Gil dumped his armload of wood into the wrought iron holder beside the enormous stone fireplace that was the centerpiece of Mac's living room. "Rots to be you, don't it?"

Mac dropped his own wood, then bent down to arrange

a fire. "Pastor Dave was dead-on casting you as the villain. You're just plain mean. You'll probably scare the little kids or something."

"Emily's delighted," Gil said as he settled into one of the large leather chairs that stood in front of the fireplace. Emily had wound up being Mary, and was over-the-top happy about her starring role, not to mention Gil's. "For all I know, she put Dave up to it."

Mac struck a match to a pile of kindling. "Who knew you had an artistic side? It's almost unnatural." He cast a sideways look back at Gil as he opened the pizza box that sat on the coffee table between them. "I can't quite see you in a crown and flowing robes. This ought to be fun."

"Speaking of unnatural, I heard you got to play hero to Mary Thorpe earlier this week. Peter Epson was telling Emily about it—said he wanted to do an article, but he was afraid his dad would throw a fit." Peter Epson was Howard's son and a reporter for the local paper.

"You see," Mac elaborated as he pointed the tip of his pizza slice at Gil, "that's exactly why I'm running. People do things—or don't do things—way too much based on what Howard will think. Okay, Peter may be a bit of an exception, but you know what I mean. The guy's got too much influence. And I don't even think he goes after half of it. You might be surprised to hear I don't actually hate Howard. Not at all."

Gil raised an eyebrow as he bit into his own slice. "Could have fooled me."

"Granted, he's overblown, self-centered, backward-looking, but this 'mayor for life' thing has gotten so out of proportion that Howard doesn't have to look at something before people *decide* how he feels about it. Okay, maybe he's grabbed at power with both hands, but we've been handing him more and more over the years without even thinking about it."

"And you're just the guy to turn us around," Gil guessed with his mouthful.

"I'm just the guy God asked to do the job," Mac clarified, meaning it. It bugged him that people thought he had it out for Howard personally, when he just wanted to change people's mind about the inescapability of Howard being mayor.

"Howard might say the same thing."

"Enter the blessings of democracy."

"Man, you really are starting to sound like a politician." Gil took a swig of his soda. "But a snake charmer? Did you and Curly really pull a milk snake out of that lady's sink?"

"The press *should* have been there. I was heroic. An epic battle. The thing was six feet long."

Gil shot Mac a dark look. "Janet Bishop said it was a foot and a half at most and it took you four minutes."

"Four very dramatic minutes. You should have heard Mary Thorpe shriek."

"She's from *Chicago*," Gil said as if it explained everything.

"Cut the woman a little slack."

Gil grinned. "Sounds like you already did. Dinah told me you bought her a nice soothing beverage afterward in the bakery. Charmer, like I said."

"She was afraid to go back into her kitchen just yet. What was I supposed to do? Just leave her standing in the hallway? After all, Curly likes her."

"Just Curly?"

"We're not in the same place, Gil. She's just barely getting her feet underneath her where her faith is concerned. I admit, she shows some spine, and…maybe under different circumstances…but not now." She wasn't Mac's type, even with those eyes.

"Circumstances change all the time. Maybe she's just what you need." Gil raised an eyebrow.

"What I need," Mac declared narrowing his eyes, "is for people to stop planning my life for me, thinking I need what everyone else *thinks* I need. God and I can tackle my own path just fine, so leave it, okay?"

"Yeah," uttered Gil, drawing out the word with a sarcastic flourish, "we'll just leave it. For the moment."

"We'll just leave it, period."

Stop it, Mary scolded herself as she felt her pace slowing. There was no reason to be afraid of opening her apartment door. Nice people were behind it. Nice people who'd asked her to a local party, to be friendly. Why is it, Mary asked herself as she caught her scowling reflection in the hallway mirror, that "nice" is so hard for you to get used to? Very pleasant people live in Chicago. You just never seemed to meet any of them. Pausing for a second to apply a friendly smile to her face, Mary put her hand on the door handle. She was about to check through the peephole when she heard Emily's voice call out "Mary, it's us!"

As if Emily suspected she had checked the peephole. Suddenly, instead of feeling like a smart, keep-yourself-safe city girl, Mary felt like a suspicious, overly cautious wimpy girl. It played in her head like an advertising slogan or a 1950s B-movie trailer: "She Came from Planet Mean."

These people have been nothing but wonderful to you. You should be thanking God every second for bringing you here. She squared her shoulders and tugged the heavy wooden door open.

And saw a wall of pine needles.

Two seconds later, that wall of needles tilted off to one side to reveal Emily Sorrent, dressed fit for a Christmas card in a fuzzy white beret, scarf and mittens. Beaming. "Surprise! I told you we'd get a tree in here! Up the stairs and everything."

The tree tilted farther to reveal a sadly resigned Gil and Mac, looking like they'd put up every inch of resistance they had to this little holiday stunt. Emily evidently was as stubborn as Dinah said. Mary didn't think too many people in Middleburg got away with bossing Gil Sorrent and Mac MacCarthy around. Especially when it meant hauling a cumbersome Christmas tree up a narrow stairway.

Mac blew a lock of hair out of his face and craned his neck around a branch. "Can we get this thing settled before the sap starts to run?"

Gil angled the trunk he was holding in through the door while Mac wrestled the top through the arched doorway. "A five-foot tree would have done, Emily," he noted, working to coax the tip under the lintel as pine needles showered everywhere.

"This apartment has lovely high ceilings," Emily defended, tugging off her mittens. "A shorter tree would have looked silly."

Gil set the trunk down onto the floor and straightened up with a groan. "A shorter tree would have weighed less, not that it mattered or anything." His voice said it mattered a great deal, but there was still a hint of humor in his eyes as he looked at his wife.

Mary was still standing there, holding the door open, probably holding her mouth open, as well. When Emily said she would fix her up with a tree, Mary didn't think she really meant it. It was just a nice thought, a pleasant thing to say. They weren't friends or anything; they'd barely met, and already Emily had given her the beautiful blue glass ornament. "I can't remember the last time I had a tree," Mary reminisced, wishing there wasn't quite so much astonishment in her voice. "Actually, I don't think I've ever had a tree of my own."

Emily looked genuinely shocked, which made sense. The woman probably started planning her Christmas decorations in July if the store's holiday abundance was any indication.

"That's horrible. Next thing you'll be telling me is that you don't have a stocking to hang over that lovely fireplace."

Mary started to say something, but Gil gave her a look and a barely perceptible head shake that silently warned, don't get her started.

"Oh, no," Mary lied. "My mom sent my stocking from home just yesterday." Note to self: get stocking from Mom ASAP.

"Well," said Mac, brushing the last of the pine needles off his jacket, "where do you want to put this thing?"

How should I know? Mary was grateful for an on-the-spot brainstorm. "Emily, where do you think?"

It took Emily about four seconds to decide that in the corner by the front windows was the best place for Mary's first-ever tree. "That way people from the street can see your lights and decorations."

"Uh…sure," Mary agreed. Second note to self: ask Janet to secretly deliver some lights, look up Christmas decorations for beginners on the Internet tomorrow morning. Where was this simple country life everyone kept talking about? Life in Middleburg kept getting more complicated by the minute.

As the men maneuvered the tree into place, Mary stood beside Emily and whispered, "You didn't tell me Mac was coming." She didn't like the evening's sudden "double date" atmosphere.

"Well, Gil couldn't get the tree up here by himself, and I didn't think you'd mind."

Gil looked plenty big enough to bring the tree up on his own, and she wouldn't have minded a three-foot tree if it would have gotten her out of this.

Her reluctance must have shown, for Emily furrowed her brows and said, "Mac was going to be there anyway. We just asked him to make a detour to help us out. He's in his own car and everything—he won't even be riding with us to the high school." The corner of her mouth turned up in a wry smile. "I'm not fixing you up." She looked back at the pair as they planted the trunk into the tree stand Emily had handed off to Gil. "Yet." With a wink, she stepped toward the tree. "Gil, it's not straight. About half a foot to the left."

Mary watched, dumbfounded yet she was moved, as Emily gave orders adjusting the tree this way and that. Someone had gone far out of their way to do something nice, completely unsolicited and certainly unexpected, for her. It did something to the pit of her stomach that she couldn't quite keep under control. She was spending her first Christmas on her own, as a believer, in her new home, and it was starting to actually *feel* like a home. The sight of the bare tree looked glorious to her, even though she was sure it looked sadly incomplete to Emily. "It's beautiful," Mary claimed resolutely. "Really." She shook Gil's hand. "Thank you so much."

"Don't thank me," he countered gruffly. "Thank Madame Holiday over there. She's got three up at the farm already, and she was threatening me with a fourth until she remembered you didn't have one yet. I ought to be thanking you."

Mary felt a laugh bubble up inside her. "Enthusiastic, hmm?"

"That don't even begin to cover it." He leaned in. "Just let her run it out, okay? If she comes back tomorrow with doodads and fake snow, just let her. I'd consider it a personal favor. The guys on the farm are pretty much at their limit."

"I'll take one for the team," Mary joked, liking how it felt. Based on what she'd heard about Sorrent's burly farmhands, she could barely imagine them choking on cinnamon potpourri and tangling in miles of red velvet ribbon.

"Much appreciated." It was the first time she saw Gil Sorrent smile.

"What are you two all whispering about?" Emily asked, returning from the kitchen with the ornament Mary had hung in the window. She'd come with one of those fancy ornament hooks Mary had seen in her shop, which she now held out to Mary with great ceremony.

"I was just giving her tree care instructions," Gil informed. "When to water and all."

"Good idea," Emily concurred. "Okay now, Mary, you do the honors."

The size of the lump in Mary's throat was just plain insane as she selected a bough and hung the single blue ornament on the tree. It was the most ridiculous thing ever. She wasn't about to let on to anyone that she'd just hung her one and only ornament on her first-ever Christmas tree. "Perfect," Mary gulped out, trying to sound ordinary even though she felt foolish and exposed.

Everyone took a second to admire the single ornament,

even though it wasn't much of an admirable display. Mary was reminded that nothing in the world smelled like a fresh Christmas tree. A dozen classic carols rang through her memory, and she thought she'd gobble up the first candy cane she could get her hands on. Would Dinah teach her to bake Christmas cookies? If not, there were sure to be plenty within easy reach with the bakery only steps away.

"We should get going," announced Mac, checking his watch. "You know how that place fills up."

Gil and Emily had offered to take Mary to the high school choral Christmas program. It sounded like one of those classic student music programs, where the freshman band struggled their way through various arrangements of holiday music, the choirs and soloists showed their young talent, and parents stood in crowds of camera flashes and video-cam tripods. Where she came from, those types of things were a relatives-only kind of affair, but here in Middleburg it seemed the whole town turned out. That may have had something to do with the "cookie walk" afterward—an event she'd never seen before but everyone seemed to find very ordinary. Hordes of people baked their best Christmas cookies, patrons paid $10 for a box to fill to the brim with whatever goodies caught their eye, and the profits bought things like band uniforms and new sheet music. With a degree in classical music, Mary found the whole thing very intriguing—even before frosting was involved. Did high school choirs still do the "Halleluiah Chorus" at the end of every Christmas concert?

Well, she thought as she wound her scarf around her neck and took a last happy look at the new tree in her living room, there's only one way to find out.

Chapter Six

Mary was just wedging a final almond snowball cookie into the corner of her box when she heard Mac's voice over her shoulder. "Excellent use of space. You've done this before."

She laughed. Not a centimeter of cookie box had gone to waste, and she'd had fun plotting just how to get as many cookies as she could for her $10 box. When Sandy Burnside had mentioned most cookies froze quite well—supposedly explaining why she was holding no less than three full boxes—Mary seriously considered investing in a second box. A tug at her tight waistband, however, lent her the necessary restraint. "I did make the most of my box, didn't I?"

Mac's box looked rather scientifically stuffed, as well. "Hey, it's for a good cause."

Mary took a sip of her punch. "I don't think my sweet tooth qualifies as a noble effort."

"Oh, no," Mac replied, "we do our ethical sugar-bingeing very well here in Middleburg. Cookies for charity have a long and delicious history in this town. I could tell you stories that could put you off peanut butter forever."

Mary sat back on one hip, selecting half a candy-cane cookie from the platter of broken "freebies" that was at the center of the cookie tables. "I'm still getting used to lots of things about Middleburg."

They moved to the cash register while Gil and Emily were still stuffing the eight boxes it took to feed Home-stretch Farm's many mouths. "Look," Mac explained, "I feel weird about the tree thing. That was sort of pushy. I thought we should have asked first, but, well, you know Emily. You looked a little taken aback about it. I feel bad."

"It was a surprise," Mary admitted, "I guess I'm just not used to people going to trouble like that for me. I feel...I don't know, indebted? I don't even know if Christmas trees are expensive."

Mac looked at her. "You don't have an ornament to your name, do you? No decorations, none of that stuff?"

Mary actually felt her eyes shift side to side, as if she were letting a secret slip. "I could pull off a string of popcorn given an hour or two." She suddenly remembered. "I've got six Christmas CDs—do they count?"

"Emily's gonna have a field day with you. You should let her. She needs a place to put her imagination these days, and I'm pretty sure their living room can't hold another nativity scene. You were smart to give her the role of Mary in the play."

"I don't need to be Middleburg's Christmas charity case." She meant it as a joke, but it wasn't that far from the truth. Even though everyone was treating her like some great answer to prayer, she felt like a fraud—like Middleburg hadn't realized what they were getting in the bargain.

Mac fished money out of his wallet as the Junior Class Glee Club tied up his purchases. "Don't think of it that way. To put it in engineering terms, Emily's like a great big pressure valve. All that holiday stuff builds up, and it needs somewhere safe to go. She got a jump start on it this year, and both the shop and the farm are all decked out. We still have weeks to go, and she needs a new target. The Christmas play and your empty apartment are just great targets. Gil'd probably thank you if you just let her run wild on your place."

"Actually," commented Mary, pulling out her own money, "he already did. Said he'd consider it 'a personal favor' if I'd let her 'snow all over me.'"

Mac grinned. "You should. That way everyone wins. You get a winter wonderland, MCC gets your full attention on the drama and Gil gets one square inch without mistletoe all over it. Emily can get obsessive. I'd sic her on my own personal holiday dilemma if I could, but I don't think it's her style."

"Holiday dilemma? Your decorations not up to snuff?"

"No, it's actually a bit more complicated than that. Or maybe just expensive. The deal is, I'll be the biggest Grinch in history if I don't get my hands on one of those ridiculous blue bears for my nephew. Pressure's on, and Uncle Mac had better come through."

"You mean a Bippo Bear?"

Mac's grin all but faded. "Man, what I wouldn't do with five minutes alone with those idiots who do this to kids at Christmas. Deliberate shortages. A gazillion ads but no product. Setting little kids up for disappointment at Christmas. It ought to be a felony. I reckon this may end up costing me $500, and that's wrong on so many levels."

"Advertising people are just doing their job. The people who make Bippo Bears need jobs, too. And the people who ship them and work in the stores that sell them. Christmas hasn't gotten so out of whack just because of Bippo Bears. That's not a fair thing to say."

"You know what's not fair? Sitting watching some harmless cartoon with my nephew when the eleventh commercial with that mind-numbing Bippo Bear song comes on, and he knows it by heart. And he looks at me with those enormous blue eyes of his and says 'Uncle Mac, I just gotta have a Bippo Bear for Christmas.' And I already know that every store within a hundred miles of here is long out and can't get more, but they're still running that ad. He's still singing that song. *That's* not fair."

"Life isn't always fair." It sounded like a tired retort—the kind of thing best left to T-shirts.

"No one should have to learn that at *five*." Somehow, he'd realized how worked up he'd gotten, and Mary could see him force calm back into his voice, pressing his shoulders down from where they'd gotten hunched up. "Twenty-five, maybe. Fifteen if girls are involved. But not five."

Mary couldn't think of too many single men who'd get so worked up over a nephew's Christmas list. Most of the men she'd known had Olympic medals in self-absorption, whose holiday or birthday present expeditions never went farther than the gift-card stand at the mall. The thought of Mac hunting down a Bippo Bear in the darkest recesses of Internet commerce was an oddly compelling picture. He'd be genuinely mad if he failed. It showed in his eyes.

Mac took a step back and wiped his hands down his face. "I'm sorry. It's not your fault, I didn't need to blast you with my frustration. I just want Christmas to be about the baby Jesus for Robby, not about Bippo Bears." He shifted his weight, making an effort to change topics. "On the other hand, I do have an issue that might actually *be* your problem."

Mary wasn't sure she wanted to know what that was. "My problem?"

"Tell me Joseph doesn't really have to wear a dress?"

Mary had to laugh. "It's a *tunic*. And while it's technically not pants, I wouldn't call it a dress, either. No knees involved whatsoever."

"I know Joseph was a carpenter, but you always see him holding a shepherd's crook. I get to hold a big stick, right? I need something to keep up with Gil's armor. And you're giving the guy minions. That's not safe."

"Gil comes with his own minions, though, so it was smart casting. And this isn't about who carries the biggest stick."

"Honey," drawled Mac, grinning and taking the twang in his accent up a few notches, "in this town it's always about who carries the biggest stick. Y'all better figure that out right now." He leaned in as they made their way back to where Gil and Emily were finishing up their purchases. "Howard doesn't get a stick as narrator, but does he get one as God?"

Mary laughed harder. "You really have brought this down to a highly personal level, haven't you?"

He didn't answer, just stood there, smiling.

"God gets a very big book, but no stick. The narrator has no props at all. I guess I'd better think long and hard before I decide which props you get. Wouldn't want it going to your head or anything."

Gil came in on the last of the conversation. "Mac? Something going to his head? Can't be done. This fella's big head is already at capacity." He adjusted the six boxes in his arms. "Matter of fact, I've been thinking if he becomes mayor, his head just might explode."

Mac narrowed his eyes at Gil. "You'd like that, wouldn't you?"

"Nah." For a minute it looked like Gil might cuff Mac—

they were like brawling brothers, those two. "Then I'd probably be the one stuck cleaning it up."

Emily came holding two more boxes of cookies. "We're done here, aren't we, boys? I've got a big day at the shop tomorrow and I'm sure Mary could do without the 'Gil and Mac Parade of Manliness.'"

In the five seconds it took them to get their dander up, Emily was practically out the door with Mary close behind. "Sorry you had to see that," Emily apologized, nodding her head back toward the pair of men. "Usually they save it for the barn." She parked the boxes on the hood of the big green Homestretch Farm truck and fished in her pocket for her car keys. "Gil said you might need help decking out your apartment for the holidays now that you've got a tree. I've got a few extra ideas if you'd like…"

"Sure," Mary conceded, wondering if she'd regret it. "I need all the help I can get."

Later that night, Mary picked out a holiday CD, heated up a mug of instant cocoa and sat a big pillar candle in the fireplace. Wrapping herself in a large fuzzy throw, she turned off all the lights and sat on the floor leaning up against the sofa. It was starting to feel like a real Christmas.

Her first Christmas away from the retail version of Christmas. Away from the professional caroling of her musical training, away from the check-the-sales-records competition of the ad career, away even from the old Mary for whom church was something people just did on Easter and Christmas. She began to hum "Away in a Manger," thinking of the baby Jesus with new poignancy. Mac was right, nothing could be further from Bippo Bears than that starlit night. "A night," as Pastor Dave had said in a recent sermon, "that split history in two. That split the universe into 'before and after' and made the impossible possible."

You have, haven't You? I'd have thought it impossible to be here. To be gone from that world and into this one. You've changed my life, and You'll always be changing it, won't You?

So why am I still so afraid? I'm glad to be using my talents for You now, here, but what do I do about all that stuff from my past? Do I throw it away, erase it like I want to? What if my past is coming after me, Lord? I'm so new at this.

You've got to show me what to do, Lord.

Mac wasn't really sure why he needed a special rehearsal in Pastor Dave's office, but when he got the e-mail, he showed up. Script in hand, Mac knocked on the office door and entered.

To find Mary Thorpe and Howard. No Pastor Dave.

"I don't have any scenes with him," Howard objected. He'd noticed, too, evidently.

Mary stood up. "That's right. You don't. Because you two don't seem to be able to get along lately. And, you know, we need to change that." Her voice was unsteady, but determined.

Mac took a step farther into the room, realizing he'd just been ambushed. Maybe he should have left the snake under the sink. "We get along just fine."

"We disagree on several issues," Howard stated formally, "but that's all."

Mary motioned to the chair at the meeting table across from Howard. "What will it take for you two to come out in favor of a community Christmas Eve potluck dinner?"

"A what?" Howard asked at the same moment Mac was thinking it.

"A community Christmas Eve dinner. A potluck. After the drama. Instead of everyone heading off to their own homes, I'm proposing we have a town-wide potluck."

"On Christmas Eve?" Mac had a long tradition of spending Christmas Eve in the privacy of his own quiet home, not surrounded by Jell-O salad and casseroles. "Don't you think it's a bit much?"

"I have to say, I'm siding with MacCarthy on this one. I admire your commitment and creativity, but I think the drama will be more than enough."

"The drama only provides limited interaction," she declared firmly. "And, only for those in the cast and crew at that. While I've made the production as big as possible, that hardly includes the whole town. Pastor Dave and I have talked it over, and we think this is just the ticket."

"Dave thought this was a good idea?" Howard's scowl matched the one Mac was trying to hide.

"He did." Mary stood her ground. "But he also said we'd get nowhere if you weren't behind it, Howard."

Howard always looked like he found that surprising, which was funny, because Mac knew Howard expected to be consulted. On everything.

"That may be true," Howard consented, "but I doubt people are going to want to spend their Christmas Eve dinners in the church basement. Folks have family. Traditions. I'm not keen to mess with that."

Normally, "messing with tradition" would be just the kind of argument to get Mac in favor of something, but not in this case. "Maybe after the dress rehearsal? You know, the night before?"

"That's not the night for it," Mary replied. "The old saying 'bad dress rehearsal, good performance' didn't come out of nowhere. This needs to be a celebration, 'job well done' and such in order to help the community come together." She spread her hands on the table. "You hired me to achieve a goal, and I think this is the way to achieve that goal. You two play a very big part in what this town is going through, that's why we cast you in such visible roles. Think of this as an extension of that."

"No offense, Mary," said Mac, "but I just don't think it's a good idea. Folks will want to be home. *I* want to be home. I have plans already, and I imagine most other people do, too."

Howard crossed his arms over his chest. "I'm just not ready to say yes to this, Miss Thorpe. And that's the truth of it."

If Mary Thorpe had done nothing else for Middleburg, she'd just come up with the one thing he and Howard could agree on.

"Will you think it over?" Mary persisted.

"I doubt I'll change my mind," Howard offered, leaning back in his chair.

"But you will think it over?" Mary definitely wasn't backing down. Where was *this* woman when the snake was in her kitchen? Mac felt a twinge of guilt for pegging her as a "fraidy cat."

"If you insist."

"I insist." Mary held Howard's eye for a moment before turning to Mac. "And you?"

"I'm with Howard. I'm no fan, but I'll give it a day or two."

"I suppose I can't ask for more than that now, can I?"

Mary shut the door behind her two targets, letting out the breath she'd been holding half of the meeting. While she hadn't gotten yes, she hadn't gotten no, either—yet.

Shaking the jitters out of her shoulders, Mary saw Pastor Dave peering around the corner. "So," he prompted, one eyebrow raised but a glint in his eye, "what happened?"

"They don't like it." Mary wasn't quite sure how she came to be disappointed in this, but maybe it was that she just hated friction between people—it was one of the reasons she'd always freelanced in her music and advertising; she just couldn't stand the "creative tension" that seemed to be the necessary evil of those kind of workplaces.

"Well, we knew that would happen. Were you able to keep them from saying an outright no? That's really as far as I reckon we were going to get, anyway."

"They said they'd think about it." That hardly qualified as a success in her book. It just barely edged its way out of the realm of failure.

"That's great!" He clasped a friendly hand on her shoulder, and broke into a wide smile. Well, at least "the boss" was pleased. "That's a victory, Mary. We'll bring 'em around, just you wait. Besides," he leaned in and whispered, "I've got our secret weapon all lined up. It's time to bring in the big guns."

Mary gulped. "Big guns?"

"Have you met Sandy Burnside?"

It was hard for anyone within six miles of Middleburg *not* to meet Sandy Burnside? "Yes."

"I got Sandy on board last night. Sandy is pretty much a force of nature around here. Between Sandy and her buddies, Mac and Howard don't stand a chance. We'll have our potluck up and running by the end of the week."

"They didn't look especially fond of the idea, Dave."

"Of course not. But that's the beauty of a small town like Middleburg." He practically winked. "There's nowhere to hide."

Chapter Seven

Mac was answering an e-mail full of campaign-issue questions from Peter Epson when Sandy Burnside burst into his office. If the woman had anything close to "downtime," Mac never saw it. He'd often wondered why Sandy had never run for mayor—she had locked horns with Howard more than anyone. She plunked down her enormous handbag on Mac's desk, nearly scattering the papers. "Why are you raising such a stink about something as sweet as Christmas Eve dinner?"

Pushing his keyboard away, Mac crossed a foot over one knee and resigned himself to whatever venting was about to come his way. "Sandy, I don't like the idea. But I'm guessing you already know that."

Sandy blew out a breath, shaking her head. "You'd think we had moved Christmas to February the way you two are hollering. Howard was breaking out the hundred-dollar phrases like 'disruption of family traditions.' 'Casualizing of an important night.'" She leaned in. "I ask you, is 'casualizing' even a word?"

"Listen, Sandy…" How he spent Christmas Eve was his

business. He didn't like that it had now become a campaign issue.

Sandy was on a roll. "And wasn't it Howard's idea in the first place to create a holiday drama that would bring the town together? I mean it wasn't actually his idea…I think it was Pastor Dave's to be exact…but doesn't Howard think every good idea was his idea?"

"Howard does like the drama thing. But we both think the dinner's too much. Howard thinks we all ought to go home and be with our families."

"Be with your family with everybody's families," Sandy countered. "All together. That's the whole point."

"Howard thinks the play will be enough and believe it or not, Sandy, I agree with him."

She shot him a *Why do you think I'm here?* glare.

"People have Christmas Eve traditions." He tried another tactic, since her expression wasn't softening one bit. "What about your schedule—aren't your stores open late on Christmas Eve?"

Sandy narrowed her eyes. "Burnside employees," she said gravely, "go home to their families at four o'clock on Christmas Eve."

"See? It's the same thing. People might want to be home. *I* want to be home."

"Getting out of work is different than saying you won't celebrate Christmas Eve with your friends and neighbors." Sandy planted her hands on Mac's desk. "We need unity."

Mac tried to keep his sigh from becoming a grunt. "I'm doing the drama thing, Sandy. I spend Christmas Day surrounded by family and kids and presents and ham and eggnog. Has it ever occurred to you that Christmas Eve is a time I like to be on my own? Quiet? In prayer even?

You're saying I'm a poor citizen—a poor Christian—because I don't want to spend that time over ground beef with people I see every other day of the year?"

Sandy's face took on a look that was far too close to pity. "You prefer to spend Christmas Eve alone?" Her tone was that of *What kind of a sick soul are you, anyway?*

There it was; that annoying *you can't possibly be happy* attitude. That look Ma got that declared a single man couldn't really be happy, only deluded or a very good liar. As if solitude or freedom were things real men outgrew. The kind of look that made Mac want to move to Montana with only cows for company. "Yes," he responded, his voice low and authoritative, "I do."

"Well," Sandy interjected, snatching up her bag. "I think that's the saddest thing I've heard this week."

"Sandy," Mac continued, even though he knew better than to get into this with her, "I've spent Christmas Eve alone for the past four years, and you never thought of me as sad before. I was a fine, upstanding citizen until ten minutes ago. A man needs his solitude."

She jutted out her chin as if the thought was selfish, unpatriotic even. "A town needs unity. Especially now. And if it needs to happen by Jell-O salad, then I'll be the first to whip up a bowl. I expect you to do the same." She turned on her heels and left his office.

Mac sat back in his chair, raked his fingers through his hair in aggravation and stared at the ceiling between him and Mary Thorpe. You did this, he thought. We're in such different places. Faith doesn't boil down to potlucks and the way anyone spends Christmas Eve, Mary. Mary was still in the realm of spiritual blacks and whites, and he'd spent enough years on the road of faith to know the detours numbered in the thousands. There might be things she could teach him, but when a woman challenged him, Mac wanted it to be about more than a Christmas Eve potluck.

The fact that Mac was walking into a costume fitting didn't do much for his sour mood. Big blue rectangle with sleeves—those Bible-era robes didn't need tailoring. Beyond how tall he was or how long his arms were, what else did they need to know?

Everything, evidently. Mac was just about at the end of his patience by the time Audrey Lupine took enough measurements to fit him for a tuxedo. Audrey was efficient and detail-oriented, which was a big plus in librarians, but he wasn't sure tunics demanded that much attention to detail. Between that, and the four times he'd been stabbed with a pin, Mac was practically stomping his way to Mary Thorpe's office to complain about the way it had invaded his life when he heard it.

Walking by the sanctuary, Mac was startled by a clear, sweet melody overhead. A violin in the choir loft, as near as he could tell. An amazingly pure, almost ethereal tune he recognized as one of those old, classical English carols. The kind he'd heard on Christmas albums, but almost no one knew the lyrics. Something that sounded as if it should be echoing in an Italian cathedral rather than through the rafters of MCC.

It was almost a minute before he realized it must be Mary—he didn't know anyone else in Middleburg who could play the violin that well, and he remembered her orchestral background from Pastor Dave's introduction. He'd forgotten that she'd been a professional musician before coming to Middleburg. The quality of her playing stunned him, making him want to hear more. He pushed through the back doors of the sanctuary so that he was standing underneath her in the choir loft.

She finished the one song, but he heard her move to the piano and begin to play. Something jazzy and contemporary, surprising him when he recognized it as "I'll Be Home for Christmas." She began to sing, and her musicality lost its precise rigid quality, the notes dipping and sliding free in a way he felt down the back of his neck.

There was such emotion in her voice and her playing. Sadness pulled at the edges of her notes. Why wouldn't Mary Thorpe be homesick? It had to be tough to inject yourself into a completely new town at Christmas. And one not dealing well with the season at that. She'd probably expected to come into a Norman Rockwell painting, not an episode of bluegrass Jerry Springer. His first impulse was to simply slip back out the door, but that would be the cowardly thing to do. So, even as her voice took on a greater sadness, Mac made his way up the choir loft stairs until he saw her seated with her back to him at the piano. He let her finish the song, but only because something told him that she needed to get all the way through the music.

"Mary," he said quietly when the last chord had died down.

Despite his effort to be unintrusive, she practically jumped off the piano bench. "Mac!"

"I'm sorry to sneak up on you. That was beautiful." He winced inwardly, thinking that sounded dumb. "Both songs. You sing so well." Again, he thought he sounded bumbling.

She blushed. "Music major. Comes with the territory I suppose."

"You okay?" He regretted asking the minute it left his

mouth. What would he do if she said no? She sounded so emotional when she sang, so sad, and he definitely wasn't ready to get into that with her.

"Fine." She said it quickly and defiantly. In a way that broadcast she was anything but fine. They both looked down for a moment, uncomfortable. "Did you need something?"

"I was here for a costume fitting. We've finally found Curly's new song, by the way."

"Really? Who'd he take a liking to?"

"You'd get a kick out of who he likes now." He rolled his eyes. "*Someone* ought to get some enjoyment out of it."

She swung her legs around the piano bench to face him. "Who'd he choose?"

"Well," Mac began to say as he took a few steps into the choir loft and sat down in one of the chairs. "I wasn't getting anywhere with any of the other CDs you gave me, so I put the radio on to one of those stations playing all Christmas music. One song came on, and he went nuts, just like he did for the tenor guy you were playing."

"Another tenor?"

"Well, I suppose you could say that. Three of them, actually."

"Oh, the *Three Tenors?* He has good taste."

"Not exactly. More like the three rodents. Curly's taken a shine to Alvin and the Chipmunks. Believe me, the only thing worse than the chipmunks' version of that 'Christmas Time is Here' song is Curly's version. It's like cats dying." He frowned at the sheer memory of Curly's yuletide caterwauling. "I never thought I'd say this, but I prefer opera to that noise."

"Oh, my!" She was trying not to laugh. "I think that would be awful."

"No thinking about it. It *is* awful. You ought to be down-right grateful Curly isn't in the office this week. It'd turn your ears black."

"Part of me wants to hear it, and the other part of me is glad I missed it."

Mac cracked a smile. "Listen to the part that happily missed it. No one but Curly's closest kin should be sub-jected to that racket."

Mary saw he was about to go, and she didn't want to let him leave without asking one question. "Speaking of kin," she added, catching him with her voice when he shifted his weight to rise, "Why don't you think the potluck Christmas Eve supper is a good idea? I mean, no offense, but it's not like you have a family to worry about or anything." That came out all wrong. Of course Mac had family—she'd met his parents and he'd talked about siblings and nieces and nephews. But he didn't have a family of his own. "That didn't quite come out right. I'm sorry."

"No," he admitted, "but I think I know what you mean." He settled back into his seat. "And I suppose it's a fair question, seeing as I don't have a wife or children, you might reckon I'd spend Christmas Eve with my folks. The truth of the matter is that I have a very important Christmas Eve tra-dition. One I'm not thrilled to give up, if you don't mind my saying." He relaxed in his chair, crossing one long booted leg over the other in the manner of someone about to tell a story.

"Five years ago my sister Nancy got real sick around Christmas time. Just after she had my nephew, Robby, to be exact. Anyways, we'd had plans for a big Christmas Eve thing, with the first grandbaby and all. Ma was pulling out all the stops. Except it came to a screeching halt when

Nancy and the baby got sick and had to go back into the hospital. I'd come down with a bit of a cold, so I couldn't go see her or Robby, but Ma and Pa and my other sisters spent every minute there. So, instead of a big celebration, I ended up spending Christmas Eve alone. By myself."

"I'm sorry," she offered.

"Don't be," he replied. "I mean, it started out as a first-class Mac pity party, with me feeling all sorry for myself. I did feel bad at the beginning—and plenty worried about my new little nephew and all. But that's just it—that worry and feeling sorry forced me to turn to God. It turned out to be one of the most amazing nights of my life. I reckon I'd have never spent that night in front of my fire praying and reading my Bible like I did if things hadn't been as bad as they were. I'd never have remembered what an amazing gift a baby can be. Up until that night, I'd been so busy, I'd forgotten all the real stuff behind Christmas. Not that I don't love the noise and chaos of Christmas Day with my family. But I need both parts—what Ma calls my 'Silent Night' and the craziness of the next day." He looked up and caught her eyes. His eyes were straightforward and transparent; they made it easy to believe what he was saying. "So now maybe you can see why I'm in no hurry to trade that in—even for Middleburg's sake. They're *both* part of Christmas for me."

It wasn't what she was expecting. She thought she was about to be lectured about horning in on traditions or how everyone should get to celebrate in their own way—something less personal than this story. The thought of a man deliberately spending such a festive evening alone with God came as a shock of sorts. The men she'd known didn't behave that way—they just didn't run that deep.

In the music and retail advertising circles she had traveled, work went full tilt right up until Christmas Eve.

Which meant everyone who worked together spent Christmas Eve together as sort of a finish-line extravaganza. After concerts or the final stretch of retail ad campaigns, Mary had spent the last two Christmas Eves at parties that started at the office or the concert hall and went on through the night. Parties that mostly seemed about consumption—running through as much food, alcohol and money as possible. Mad dashes to find the holiday cheer that always seemed just out of reach, or the thing everyone *else* had. After all, Christmas concerts were just another workday for musicians. This past year had been particularly surreal; Thornton had gone through so much champagne that he'd tried to corner her in the coatroom of the restaurant where they were all having dinner. As a matter of fact, it had been the frantic excesses of that evening— and the emptiness of that following holiday morning—that had begun her journey back to the church. She'd been so disillusioned by the experience that on Christmas morning, she had wandered the city until she found a church service and stepped into a sanctuary for the first time since elementary school. It was one of the reasons another Christmas in the advertising business had become too much to bear.

"Too many people spend Christmas Eve alone, Mac, and not because they want it that way."

"That's probably true in a city like Chicago, but not so much here."

She couldn't let that go. "Are you so sure?"

"What do you mean by that?"

"Aside from the point about getting everyone together to celebrate the drama, don't you think there ought to be a place where people can come if they don't have somewhere else to go for Christmas Eve?" She made a point to keep the emotion out of her voice. Truth was, she suspected that without the potluck, she'd be spending Christmas Eve cleaning up after the drama so that the sanctuary was ready for Christmas morning services. Part of her knew that she'd probably get an invitation from someone in Middleburg, if not several, but another part of her worried she was too new to end up anywhere but amid boxes in the church basement.

He crossed his arms over his chest. "Well, sure I think it'd be fine to invite people to get together if they need somewhere to go. But to *make* everyone?"

"Oh, so you mean it should be some kind of last resort? A lonely hearts club for the poor souls with nowhere else to go?" He'd hit a nerve, making her feel inferior to him because she resisted a night alone during the holidays when he'd mastered his solitude.

"I didn't say that."

"Didn't you?"

"No."

"So the folks who need to get together, who haven't achieved your level of spirituality, can band together to get each other through the holiday as long as they leave you alone?"

Mac's eyes darkened into the color of stormy seas. "Hey, wait a minute. You're blowing this way out of proportion. I didn't say anything like that. I'm trying to be nice."

"Nice? By making anyone without significant holiday plans feel shallow?

"What's up with you? I came here to explain myself, and you stomp all over me."

"You came here after eavesdropping on my music. Thanks for that, by the way. How long were you down there listening? 'Both songs,' you said, right?"

He stood up fuming. "Now look here. I'm not stalking you. I was on my way to look for you when I heard you singing. I thought you sounded nice, but I didn't realize what a crime it was to compliment you. And you're way out of line on the Christmas Eve thing, if you ask me. If you want to know who's passing judgments, it's you, expecting me to ditch something important to me just because you've decided something else is more important to you. Turning Christmas Eve from a holiday into some kind of civic test I've got to pass or fail." He stormed toward the door. "You haven't lived in Middleburg long enough to know how much I don't take to being backed into a corner, ma'am. I don't. Not at all. I'll do the play, and do it gladly. But you've got me at my limit, so don't push me beyond it." He added "Please," almost as an afterthought before he ducked down the stairs.

Mary heard his heavy footsteps stomp out of the choir loft and balled her fists. How had that conversation gone from complimentary to confrontational in so short a time? She heard the sanctuary doors bang shut and decided she was glad she couldn't make out whatever it was that Mac was mumbling. She was sure it wasn't "Merry Christmas."

What happened, Lord? He'd startled her, but that wasn't grounds for jumping down his throat. He'd offered personal information, gone out of his way to explain himself. The uncomfortable truth was that he'd simply hit a nerve—the exact wrong nerve—and she'd overreacted. He couldn't know how much personal meaning Christmas Eve held for her, or that his own personal connection with the night was at odds with hers. *Oh, Lord, this is all wrong. Couldn't we be dealing with Easter? Why'd You give me the idea to host a community Christmas Eve?*

Chapter Eight

Dinah Rollings came up to Mary after the next rehearsal, putting a hand on her shoulder. "Nicely done. You handled those two well. Even the best horse trainers would have been breaking a sweat over Howard and Mac tonight."

Mary sighed, pushing the stress out of her shoulders with the breath. "They were prickly, weren't they?"

"Well, pricklier than usual." She walked with Mary through the sanctuary as they began shutting off the banks of lights. "This mayor thing is turning out a whole lot more complicated than anyone thought it'd be. I give Mac credit, though, for doing it at all. Most of us wouldn't have had the nerve."

"It's my fault," Mary conceded. "It's asking a lot of him to spend Christmas Eve at the church."

Dinah stopped and turned to look at Mary. "You are not. You're asking him to rethink ideas and take hold of a better one. I think the Christmas Eve thing is a fabulous idea— course, you already know that. But the way I see it, you're not asking anything different than he's asking of the town to think about voting him in as mayor." She furrowed her brow for a moment, considering. "Come to think of it, that may be why it bugs him so much. Cuts a little too close to home."

"No one wants to get stressed out at Christmas."

"And no one wants to be alone—okay, maybe except for Mac, but we already know he's odd. I mean, look at that bird. The guy needs a normal pet, don't you think?"

Mary laughed. "Well, that may have had something to do with it, too. I don't think it's done wonders for Mac's stress level to have Curly belting out nonstop opera. And now…"

"Culture's good for guys." She hesitated for a moment. "And what do you mean by 'and now'?"

Mary shut off the last of the lights. "He hasn't told you?"

"I haven't talked to him much this week. Come on, what's behind the 'and now,' Mary?"

"Mac's been playing the radio to try and find Curly something new to sing. Well, Curly found something, but even Mac'd consider it worse than the first."

"Curly's got a new song, hm?"

"The Chipmunks' 'Christmas Song.'" It really was hysterical when you thought about it. Every time Mary tried to imagine Curly's screeching tenor rendering the squeaky, cheesy tune, she burst out laughing. If she didn't think he'd find it so offensive, Mary would have asked for a command performance.

Dinah's eyes grew wide. "No. You're kidding!"

"That's what he said."

Dinah erupted into giggles alongside Mary. "That's rich. That's just priceless. Oh, I think I'd pay to hear that. I might even pay to watch Mac listen to that."

"Don't ask him. Please. It'd just make things worse."

"Oh, I don't know. This is just so delicious. Curly. Singing chipmunks. I couldn't make this stuff up. Oh, Mary, you just made my day. And don't worry about Mac. He and Howard will get over themselves in time to get everyone on board for Christmas. And you've got me— and Janet, and Emily—on your side. That's got to be worth *three* grumpy mayors at least."

They'd reached Mary's office and she locked up for the night. "Thanks. I hope you're right."

"I am. You just stick to your guns."

Mary looked up from the box of props she was sorting when she heard the knock on the church storage room door. The last person Mary expected to see in the open doorway when she looked up was Howard Epson. "Hard at work, I see?" he said a little stiffly.

"Lots to do," she proclaimed, pushing the box back into its place on the shelves. "Nice to see you, Howard."

"Do you have a moment, Miss Thorpe?" he asked formally, officially. As if he'd prefer to have this conversation somewhere more conventional than a storage room.

"Please, you can call me Mary. I was just on my way to the kitchen for some coffee. May I pour you a cup? We can talk in my office." She still loved being able to say that phrase "in my office." Freelancers and musicians just didn't have offices. Most of her work got done on her kitchen table, in ad agency conference rooms and in rehearsal halls. It felt marvelously homey to have even the tiniest of offices.

"That'd be fine."

They collected their coffees and settled into Mary's small office. "Mary," Howard spoke, setting his mug down on her desk carefully, "I've come to talk about the Christmas Eve potluck." His manner had become, if possible, even more official. She wondered, at that moment, if she'd ever seen him laugh. Smile, yes, but she couldn't recall hearing the big old man laugh.

"I figured you had," she offered, trying to sound as encouraging as possible. His formality was more than a bit intimidating. Did he know that and wield it, or was it just an unavoidable by-product of his take-charge personality?

He adjusted the buttons on the cardigan sweater— standard grandfather issue to go along with his white hair, round build and silver glasses. "I've been giving a lot of thought to this."

"I'm glad," she commented, remembering she'd asked both him and Mac to consider the idea carefully before rejecting it outright as they seemed ready to do. "Please, go ahead."

"I feel a certain obligation," Howard began, folding his hands across his lap, "toward your success here. It was my idea to bring you on board because I felt this town was in grave danger of a deep division. One of the reasons we're investing in this little drama is to help renew the town's community spirit. I take this town's best interests to heart every day. I take my mayoral calling very seriously."

That was obvious. "I'm sure you do. I think that says a lot about you, Howard. And a lot about Middleburg."

"So I've decided that a higher level of civil service is required. I've prayed about this, long and hard, and I've decided that if I'm serious about my commitment to town unity, if I started this by bringing you here and if you believe this potluck is going to achieve that goal…well then, I'd be a hypocrite if I didn't sacrifice my family's private celebrations for the greater good."

He pronounced the words as if she'd asked him to undertake a suicide mission. He looked down and folded his hands across his lap with grave resignation. Howard was so tremendously, deeply serious that she didn't dare smile, even though she found his attitude a bit absurd. It was, after all, just a holiday potluck supper.

But Howard—and half of Middleburg, for that matter—didn't see it that simply.

"Howard, I admire your willingness to give this a try." She tried to make her voice as formal as Howard's even though it felt foolish. "I think that's very…civic of you. I appreciate it more than you know. I'm sure you won't regret it."

"It's my prayer that you're right, Miss Thorpe. The last thing this town needs is another reason to argue. Especially at Christmas."

"I appreciate that, sir." Mary didn't know where the urge to call him sir came from, but he seemed to like it. "I'll do my best to make good on the trust that you've given me."

His declaration made, Howard rose and took his coat from where he'd folded it across the back of his chair. "Middleburg is an astounding place, Miss Thorpe. A rare, wonderful place." She could see that he meant every dramatic word. The man really loved his hometown.

Mary extended her hand warmly. "I hope I come to love it as much as you do, Howard. I'm sure I will."

"See you at rehearsal." He shook her hand with a public official's firm grip. "I've all my lines memorized already, ahead of schedule."

As God/Narrator, Howard had no need to memorize his lines as he would "read" his part out of a giant prop Bible. She'd told him that, twice, but she swallowed her point and smiled. "That's wonderful."

"Good day."

It wasn't until he'd left the room that Mary realized he'd never touched a drop of his coffee. What an odd, surprising fellow Howard Epson was.

Mac hit Enter, thinking there was something supremely wrong with the world when a grown man paid that much money for a blue singing teddy bear. He knew Bippo Bears were just the fad of the hour, and that if he went over to his sister's house in January and asked Robby to show him his Bippo Bear, the boy might not even remember where he put it. Mac knew all this. He knew the evils of consumerism, he knew the craving was purely a profit-seeking game the toy retailers played every year. None of that stopped him from doing whatever it took to make Robby happy. Maybe it was that they'd come so close to losing him on his first Christmas. Mac could just never stomach the thought of disappointing that boy at the holidays. His role was indulgent Uncle Mac, and maybe that was best. Mac, you have no spine. You'd make a lousy parent.

He shut down his computer and closed up the office for the day. After an errand or two, he'd settle down for a relaxing night memorizing the last of his lines for the play. Curly had fallen off his passion for chipmunk tunes, and things were feeling almost normal around his house. As a matter of fact, Ma had only harped on him once this week about his approaching thirtieth birthday.

His birthday. Only weeks away now. It did bug him that he was turning thirty, but not in the way others seemed to think it did. He wasn't having some sort of benchmark-year crisis, but he didn't want to enter his fourth decade on earth just sliding into some bland expected path. He'd always felt wired differently than everyone else—as if doing things differently were part of his nature. And while other folks might think of that as odd, Mac thought of it as being equipped for God's more unique tasks. He could take more heat, swim upstream, go against the grain and be creative better than anyone he knew. Someone like that just doesn't do the "settle down with a spouse and kids and an Irish setter" lifestyle that his sister had done. He loved Robby, but always thought he was more suited for the adventurous bachelor uncle than any kind of stable homestead.

He walked down the street toward Bishop Hardware, admiring the Christmas tree in the park along Ballad Road as he went. The town really was at its best for the holiday season. The season's first snowfall was forecast, and it would just dust everything with a painting-worthy coat of white. The place would look like a Christmas card scene over the weekend. Not only was that nice to look at, it brought the tourists out in droves, and tourists spent money. Charming weather meant chiming cash registers, and Mac knew many of the retailers in town were counting on a good holiday season this year.

He was just finishing his purchase when he caught sight of Mary Thorpe in the aisle where Janet kept her small selection of Christmas lights. They hadn't left things well at their last encounter, and he couldn't decide whether or not to get back on better terms. She'd jumped down his throat. Then again, he'd done whatever the musical version of eavesdropping could be called.

She walked up to him. "Hey, Mac." She had a "Can we start over?" expression on her face.

"Hi. Adding to the decorations on your tree?"

She managed a smile. "No, the tree's actually pretty full. Emily's been busy. I think I've only paid for about one tenth of the stuff on my tree. She's calling it overstock, but I don't believe her."

"She loves that stuff. And she loves doing things for other people. She went a little nuts when I first moved into my house. I thought she was going to throw me one of those shower things women do, she kept bringing me so many household gadgets. I'm here to tell you, men do not need a garlic press. We smash garlic with knives." He was running on at the mouth, nervous about how they'd gotten down each other's throats so quickly at their last meeting. She made him antsy, and he wasn't used to that.

"Look," she offered, "I wasn't very nice to you the other day. I guess I'm a little wired up about this holiday and you hit a nerve or something."

"I wasn't too friendly, either. Seems there are a lot of people on their last nerve." He thought about the last customer service rep he'd talked to earlier this morning in his endless search to score a Bippo Bear for something less than three times the manufacturer's price. That poor employee sounded like she wasn't going to make it through the day, much less the remainder of the holiday shopping frenzy. "That was unfair, listening in on you like that. But really, I wasn't snooping or anything. Your voice just caught me by surprise."

"Violin, I do in public. My singing is more personal. But you couldn't have known that." She drew in a deep breath. "I'd like to make a peace offering. Pie at Deacon's? That is, if you're not busy. I'd understand if you had work to do and all. But seeing as you're already out…"

His first impulse was to decline. They seemed to be able to rile up each other too easily. Not only that, but small-town eyes would catch the two of them together, one-on-one, and might start small-town tongues to wagging. He definitely wasn't ready to give anyone reason to pair them off. Still, for all his thought of being the more "mature" in his faith, it was her extending the olive branch when he'd hesitated to do so.

She was putting in an effort, and they really did need to clear the air between them. You'd be a louse to say no, he told himself. No one in their right mind said no to pie at Deacon's, anyway—she'd picked up on the local habits right quick. "I think that'd be fine. Nothin' waiting for me back at the office but more reports, anyway. A little pie might be just the ticket to get me over what I just forked out for the nephew's Christmas present."

"Do you have any little people you have to buy for this Christmas?" Mac started the conversation as they slid into a booth at Deacon's Grill.

"My brother is married, but they're not the family type. He and his wife travel all over the world for his exporting business. No kids, no plans for kids. I don't think I'll get the chance to be an aunt anytime soon."

"Well, this year, count yourself in good standing. I just paid an unnatural sum for one of those Bippo Bears, even though I knew better. Those advertising people should have their heads examined."

She got that odd look on her face again, growing quiet. Finally, he saw her make a mental decision of sorts.

"Yeah, about that...."

"About what?"

He couldn't quite place her expression. It was a trapped, end-of-my-rope kind of look in her eyes, but then again not. A half nervousness, half ashamed, cornered look that seemed completely out of place for their circumstances.

"About the Bippo Bears. I…um…well, there's something you should know about me and Bippo Bears."

He didn't think she'd asked him out to pie to talk about Bippo Bears. What did this year's toy fad have to do with anything? Why did she have such an odd, pained look on her face?

"You're a closet Bippo Bear fan and you wanted to know where I scored mine?" He tried to lighten the mood, unsettled by how tense she was.

Mary laughed casually, but it came out a bit choked and forced. "No, not at all. It's more the other end of that."

"You're morally opposed to Bippo Bears? Or uncles splurging for unwary five-year-olds?"

At that point Gina arrived to take their order. Mac ordered his usual, with ice cream, and Mary went for the triple berry. Once Gina left, Mary spread her hands on the table. "I'm trying to figure out how to explain this. I suppose you don't even have to know, but, well, I suppose someone should know. The whole Bippo Bear thing," she went on, looking supremely uncomfortable, "well, I'm partially responsible. Actually, I feel like I'm a lot responsible. I suppose that's debatable, but not really to me."

She wasn't making sense. "Mary, what are you trying to say?"

"It's what I used to do before I came here, Mac. I wrote…" she winced on the word "…I used to write jingles, and I wrote the Bippo Bear song. The reason all those kids can sing that song endlessly to their parents? That's me. The reason you felt like you had to shell out whatever it took to buy one of those? It's me. I wrote the song, I created the frenzy."

She wasn't explaining, she was confessing. She squinted her eyes shut, as if some force would come out of the blue and knock her over for her crimes. "You? You're the evil Bippo Bear mastermind? No offense, but you just don't look the type." Sitting endlessly on hold, he had imagined the guy behind Bippo Bears as a cross between Ebenezer Scrooge and the Grinch. A slimy guy in a shiny suit punching triple-digit profits into his laptop. Not a soft-spoken blonde who barely topped five and a half feet tall.

"I'm just the mastermind behind the Bippo Bear *song*." She said it as if it would brand a scarlet *B* onto her chest.

"That silly song? That incredibly annoyingly silly song? That's yours? You wrote that?" He stared at her, still trying to put the information into some kind of context that made sense. "Well, if you're working on commission, I can see how you can afford to live on what MCC can afford to pay you." He regretted that remark the minute it left his mouth. That was a lousy thing to say. No one held a gun to your head to make you plunk down that money for that bear, Mac. You're to blame for how much you spent, not her. He'd said something wounding at a vulnerable moment. He'd done that more than once now, hadn't he? *What is it with this woman that brings out the worst in me?*

"I'm not particularly proud of myself, if it makes you feel any better." Her voice sounded definitely hurt. "Yes, I seem to be able to write tunes that stick in people's heads. I'm very good at it. And before…before I woke up to faith, as I like to put it…it didn't bother me at all, because I made a lot of money in music, which was something I loved. I had the kind of job other people dreamed about. I could do as much or as little work for the ad agency as I wanted, depending on my schedule with the orchestra. I could support myself as a musician, and not a lot of people can say that."

"I suppose that is an accomplishment. Sounds like a pretty sweet deal."

"Like most sweet deals, it tends to get to you after a while." The pie arrived, providing irony and a bit of a break in the serious nature of the conversation. Mac was having a serious conversation about Bippo Bears. It was just too odd. "Well, at least it got to me," she went on. "The funny thing is, once I realized how big Bippo Bears were going to be, once I realized what was going on and what I was helping to create, I couldn't stomach it anymore. Now that I've learned what Christmas is supposed to be about, I couldn't be part of the *buy this, buy that, put yourself in debt to give your kids ten seconds of hollow bliss* machine. That sounds simplistic, but it was like I was choking on my own work. I was getting physically ill. I couldn't sleep at night. I'd cringe anytime I heard the commercial—I still do. And so while it wasn't exactly a brilliant plan, the best thing I could do was just leave."

Mac felt like whacking his forehead. "And since you've met me, I've spent a good chunk of time railing against the sinister fiends who made little kids want Bippo Bears. Mighty hospitable of me. Look, I'm sorry. If I'd have known…"

"You'd what?"

She had him there. "Well, I might have kept my mouth shut for starters."

She eyed him, a little bit of that spine he saw over the potluck coming back. "You don't strike me as the kind of guy who holds back an opinion on anything."

"Still, I might have used nicer adjectives than 'idiotic.' You were just doing your job. You were hired to sell bears, and believe me, you're selling bears. Your little song just duped me out of a hundred and fifty dollars plus shipping and handling."

She pointed at him with her fork. "See? That's *just* why I left. Yes, I was doing my job, and people pay lip service to the idea at first, but then there comes some remark about how my song took their money. You did it yourself." Mary speared her pie with a little too much emphasis. "Most people draw a very thin line between advertising and manipulation, and I'll tell you, it's no fun living on the dark side of that line. That's why I don't tell people. That's why I had to get away." She shook her head. "The funniest thing of all is that I came to Middleburg to find someplace where all the commercialism and fighting over Christmas *didn't* reach. And I found you forking more than one hundred dollars for a Bippo Bear and a town fighting over mayors. Where's this simple life I keep reading about?"

Mac felt stung by the lecture, mostly because she was dead on. He could have easily said no to Robby's nonstop requests for the bear. Probably should have. And yet he had attached *her* talent to *his* weakness—personally—the moment he'd found out. Suddenly, her former employment didn't seem such a dumb secret to keep after all. "Simple life? Here in Middleburg? No such thing. We like to make everything complicated." He looked at her. "Why tell me? Couldn't have been my overwhelming sensitivity. I know I wouldn't have told me if I were in your shoes."

She seemed stumped by the question. "Actually, I'm not sure. Probably just to get you to stop complaining about it, I suppose. You and I do seem to have a talent for stomping on each other's last nerve." She dragged her fork through the huge dollop of whipped cream Gina had doused onto her pie. "You paid *how much* for that bear?"

"A hundred and fifty plus shipping and handling." He'd felt pained but victorious when he'd secured the bear. Now he just felt conned and stupid.

She managed a smile. "Thornton lives for people like you."

"Thornton?"

"My boss. My *ex*-boss, that is. Thornton hired me out of grad school, thinking he could get a few catchy tunes out of a music major. I can blame him for discovering my dark talent for earworms."

"Earworms? Sounds gross."

"Earworms are those tunes you can't get out of your head. Jingles, television show themes, that sort of thing. They're an incredibly powerful marketing tool because you can't get rid of them even when you want to." She pointed to herself. "And that, sir, is what I seem to be able to do better than anyone in the Midwest." Her hands dropped, and her shoulders with them. This really did bug her. She definitely classified this as a curse rather than a talent.

Suddenly he had to know. "What else have you done? Are there others I would know?"

She blushed. Actually turned crimson right there in front of him. And he realized what a mean question that was. "I mean, you don't actually have to tell me," he backpedaled. "It's your business."

She looked down at her pie for a moment, then said quietly, "Jones Bars."

"The ice cream bar?" That song had been so effective ice cream trucks had taken it up as the tune they played as they came down the street. "The ice cream truck song? Whoa, I know parents who would do you bodily harm."

She grimaced. "I got a double Christmas bonus for that

one. And a weekend in Bermuda. And then there's Paulie's Pizza."

Even his nephew could sing the Paulie's Pizza song. And yes, it was annoying. But, like she said, almost anyone could dial the Paulie's Pizza 1-800 number from memory.

"See?" she said with a lopsided, bittersweet grin, "I've got a résumé that would make your ears burn."

Chapter Nine

S he'd told him. She'd actually told someone and she hadn't spontaneously combusted. Nor, evidently, had he. He was a long way from impressed, and he definitely looked at her a bit sideways, but he hadn't up and left the room. And he had a one-hundred-and-fifty-dollar reason to hate her now that he knew. While Mary could argue with herself that this didn't rank very high on the scale of possible human secrets, she still felt like a thousand pounds had just flown off her shoulders. "I'm not proud of what I did," she admitted. "Actually, I was proud of it back then, but now it just feels, well, hollow. A lousy use of whatever talent God chose to give me." She dared to look him in the eye. "I won three awards for the pizza song, you know. And, according to Thornton, the Bippo Bear jingle has already been nominated twice. I could write my own ticket with Thornton if I wanted to go back. *If.*"

"But you don't, do you?" Mac leaned back in the booth. "Mary Thorpe, jingle star. Man, I'm not sure I could walk away from all that money and attention. I've been trying to figure out how someone like you landed someplace like this, but it sort of makes sense now." He shook his head. "Bippo Bears aren't cute, you know. They're all bug-eyed and smiley-faced." He made a disturbingly accurate impersonation of the distinctive Bippo Bear face. "No offense."

She managed a laugh. She hadn't yet been able to laugh about her former job. The last day had been so horrible with Thornton. You'd have thought he'd never lost an employee before, the way he had ranted and raved. Granted, she hadn't exactly given two weeks' notice, but this wasn't a situation that fell within the confines of normal personnel policies. Those final days, when the store orders came flooding in for Bippo Bears and the manufacturer's rep had taken her and Thornton to lunch at a very ritzy restaurant and crowed about how much money they were going to make, how desperate kids would be to get their hands on Bippo Bears, Mary had been unable to eat. From that lunch until the moment she typed up her résumé, she'd barely been able to keep anything down. And here she was, laughing about it over pie. If that wasn't God's grace showing up in her life, then she didn't know what was. "I can't believe I actually told you. I told myself I wouldn't tell…."

At that moment, as if by horrible design, the television behind Gina's counter kicked into a commercial for Bippo Bears. Mary felt the tune and lyrics as if they were physical blows. She closed her eyes and gripped the table. And waited. For the excruciating moment she knew would follow.

"See that?" a tiny voice from across the room said. She didn't even have to turn. She could picture the tiny, chubby hand pointing to the television while the other hand tugged insistently on Mommy's sleeve. "I want that. I really want that. I gotta have one, Mommy! I gotta!"

"You and every other little guy on the planet, sweetie," came Gina's voice. "Rare as hen's teeth, those are."

Mary felt the collar of her turtleneck sweater tighten around her throat.

"We'll see," warned whoever's Mommy, in that parental tone of voice everyone knows really means *No, but I'm not going to say no right now.*

She opened her eyes to find Mac staring at her. "Wow," he noted quietly, "that really gets to you, doesn't it?"

"I can't wait to have success in something less dastardly." Mary gulped down some coffee, feeling the warmth ease the ice-cold viselike grip that song had on her neck. "I used to love hearing my stuff on the television. Now it's just awful." She put down her mug, feeling the old anger rise up. "Did you know the company actually scans the Internet to find the highest current going price and sends out a press release? If they spent as much time and money on making more bears as they do on feeding the frenzy…" she didn't even finish the thought.

The child at the diner counter had now dissolved into a nonstop, earsplitting "I wanna Bippo Bear" whine. "Okay," he relented. "I can see why you might want to keep this under wraps."

"I did that," Mary confessed, inclining her head toward the drama playing out behind them.

"You did your job. And now you don't do that job anymore. You got a fresh start, and maybe that was the best choice to make if it bothers you so much."

Despite earlier frustrations, Mac had to consider it a pleasant evening. He'd scored his Bippo Bear—even if it had made him crazy and broke to do it—and patched things up with Mary Thorpe. Mac decided he couldn't complain.

Until his phone rang within thirty minutes of getting home.

"Hello, Ma," Mac greeted as he answered. "I got Robby his bear, so we're all set."

"Are we?" Ma asked in sugary-sweet tones. "Audrey Lupine just called to say she saw you and Mary Thorpe having a very serious conversation in quiet tones over at the diner. She's a pretty girl, Mary is. Anything you want to tell me?"

I love Middleburg, Mac thought to himself, but then there are days where I just hate it.

There wasn't a single empty branch on that Christmas tree. It was starting to look like a holiday catalog exploded in her living room. So when she opened her apartment door to find Emily Sorrent with three large boxes in her arms, Mary gulped. She'd thought Gil was exaggerating about Emily, but she no longer doubted the man. If she didn't think of a new target for Emily's decorating urges, she'd have trouble finding her furniture under all this.

"Emily," she began congenially as the woman deposited the boxes on her dining room table. "You've done enough. Really. More than enough."

"Oh, no, it's nothing," Emily countered, pulling the top off the first box. "Just a bit more extra stuff I've got."

"I don't think my apartment can hold much more. Look around. I think I've got more decorations than furniture."

Emily actually looked around. Mary willed her to see the abundance that was bordering on ostentation. Would it be rude to call for a yuletide intervention? "Well, I suppose there's a lot in here already, isn't there?"

Mary offered the warmest smile she could produce. "How about we have a cup of tea instead of breaking out more mistletoe? I don't need another decoration, Emily, but I'd love your company." She pulled Emily toward the kitchen.

"I decorated the church yesterday, and I had this left over. I just hated to see it go to waste."

"I'm sure you'll find a place for it. And the church looks better than most of the department stores I've seen in Chicago. I'd say you've done more than your share."

Emily settled herself into one of Mary's chairs. "I guess you're right. Gil says I should rest more than I do. But this Christmas, I just seem to be in constant decorating mode. Listen," she said, shifting a bit in her chair. "Can you tell me how you cast the drama?"

"How?"

"You know, how you decided which person should get which part."

There wasn't much to say. In fact, Mary was a bit embarrassed by her casting method. "Well, actually, I just laid the script out on my table and said a prayer each time I looked over the list. I started with the smaller parts first, and then divvied the larger parts up from a list of people Pastor Dave thought would do a good job." She'd gotten a weird feeling when she'd cast Emily as Mary, but she didn't think that was the sort of thing she ought to share. "I just made it up as I went along, I suppose."

Emily was paying very close attention to her process. "That's how you did it? You prayed?"

Now Mary felt embarrassed. It felt important to pray over her decisions when she'd made them, but now, saying it out loud, it felt rather foolish. "Well, I tried to think things through from a practical standpoint, too. I knew

Mac and Howard would need big roles based on the whole reason we were doing the drama."

"But me, you prayed before you cast me?" There was something behind Emily's questions, and Mary couldn't decipher if it was a good something or a bad something. "Really?"

"Emily, are you uncomfortable with being Mary? It's not too late to change it if you feel like you'd rather not." It was a lie—it'd be a huge problem, but the look in Emily's eyes was making her panic. Emily had looked ecstatic when she'd first found out she'd be playing Mary, which made the woman's current questioning all the more baffling.

"No, I'm really glad to be Mary."

"Is something wrong?"

"No, not at all. I just wanted to be sure before I told you."

"Told me what?"

"Why it means so much to me that you cast me as Mary. And especially if prayer was involved in your casting, because that just confirms it." Emily wasn't making a whole lot of sense, until Mary watched her hand steal protectively across her abdomen, when it suddenly made a whole lot of sense. Within seconds, Mary could easily guess what news was coming next. "I'm pregnant," Emily confided.

"That's wonderful news," Mary offered. She couldn't help but smile—the expression on Emily's face rivaled any of the twinkling lights she'd loaded onto Mary's tree.

"It's been a bit tricky, and we weren't sure when to tell everyone. I've been bursting with the news, but the doctors told us to be cautious for another couple of weeks. And then, when I could barely stand it a moment longer, you told me I'd be playing the part of Mary. I knew it was God's way of telling me everything would be okay."

It was a disorienting combination of wonderful and awful. While it felt amazing to be used by God in such an extraordinary way, Mary felt like far too much was now riding on a very minor decision. Based on Dave's information, there hadn't been that many women to play Mary—many of the other women who were suited for the role were being used in other aspects of the drama. Emily could easily be reading far too much into a decision that wasn't intended to be the portent of anything. *Oh, Lord, is this right?* "Do you think God really works that way? I mean, I know I'm new to this faith business, but…"

"I'm not saying that this makes everything fine—there's still a lot Gil and I will have to face. But yes, I do think God answers prayers for comfort, and that's what I was praying for. What I was most upset about, funny enough, was not being able to be publicly pregnant, if that makes any sense. I've waited so long to be a mom. Gil is my second husband. My first husband died before we could start a family. So when we found out, I was just exploding with the need to tell everyone, even though the doctors told us to take it slow. I wasn't coping very well. If you can believe it, I was actually more…enthusiastic… about the holiday decorating at the farm."

"Oh," said Mary, "I can believe it."

"I prayed that God would send me a way to cope with not being able to shout it from the rooftops. This is just what I needed." She looked up sheepishly. "My goodness, that sounds crazy when I hear myself say it. You must think I'm insane."

Mary could only smile. "I think you're a woman who is just very, very happy to be pregnant. And I suppose if I believe God can work through anybody, then I'd better believe God can choose to work through me. Although I'm a bit freaked out, if you really want to know. It explains a lot. I mean, in a good way. I mean…"

"It's okay. Gil's hinted that I went a bit overboard in the holiday cheer department." She paused, looking around the apartment. "I suppose I did, didn't I?"

"It's kind of nice. I feel so welcomed. I was worried I'd feel sad, that my apartment would feel empty."

Emily broke into a chuckle. "No chance of that with me around. I promise I'll take it down a notch from here on in, okay?"

He'd found her.

Mary suspected—knew down deep somewhere—that Thornton wouldn't take her exit lying down. He was a controlling sort of man, incensed when he didn't get the last word, and she'd certainly set her resignation to be just that. Despite the P.O. box and forwarding addresses she'd arranged with her parents, someone as skilled and determined as Thornton Maxwell would find a way. The fact that he'd contacted her, without her parents knowing he'd located her, just proved his ability to deceive.

And, just like Thornton would do, he'd been anything but direct. The final paycheck had arrived in an ordinary fashion, like any number of Christmas cards or electric bills mailed daily around the country.

It was her final paycheck. Hand-signed by Thornton, and mailed here, even though she'd not given the agency her Middleburg address. She'd purposely, carefully made sure the agency only had her parents' address in Illinois, and her parents forwarded her mail to a P.O. box, but Thornton had her *actual* street address. The envelope held only a check—no written message. Then again, it didn't need to. Without a word, without anything, Thornton's delivered check broadcast, "I found you."

Mary sank down on the step, too stunned to finish the flight of stairs to her apartment. He'd gone looking for her, which meant he still wanted her back, and Thornton was a man used to getting what he wanted. A man who'd built an empire on his persuasive abilities. She could imagine the lengths Thornton would go to, the incentives he would dangle, the pressure he'd apply. It was why she'd made the drastic step of running away—she wasn't sure she could withstand the full-force of the former power and money.

She set the letter down while her head sank back against the wall.

Jesus, stay beside me. You gave me the strength to walk away from all that once. Am I strong enough to keep away? Especially if it's Thornton doing the chasing? Her mind produced the verses of "O Come, O Come, Emmanuel" as if pulling them out of the fog of her memory. Emmanuel. God with us.

"Hey, are you okay?" Mary opened her eyes to find Mac staring at her from the bottom of the stairs. After a second, he dropped his briefcase at the landing and walked up the half a dozen stairs to where she lay slumped against the wall. "You are definitely not okay. Not even close." He noticed the pile of mail on the step below her. "Nasty Christmas card or something?"

"Sort of." She couldn't manage much more than that.

He looked at her. She felt like a good half of the time they'd ever spent together had been comprised of him looking baffled at her. "Should I check to see if something's ticking?"

"A bomb? Too blunt for Thornton. He's a hunter. A stalker. Explosions would be too quick and easy."

"Thornton. Your ex-boss sent you something?" He found the envelope on the top of the pile and inspected it. "Looks like an ordinary check to me."

"Exactly. That's how I know it's from Thornton. He'd know I'd know."

"I'm not getting it. Why *shouldn't* you get your final paychecks from your previous job?"

"I should, just not *here*. They don't have this address. I made *sure* they didn't have this address. All my mail from the agency is supposed to go to my parents in Illinois." Mary grimaced. "He found me."

"This guy sounds truly creepy."

"Thornton goes beyond creepy."

Mac set the envelope back down. "Look, I don't know much about the whole situation other than the little bit you've told me, but do you think you might be reading too much into this?"

A huge part of her wanted to believe him. To give Thornton the benefit of the doubt and to believe she'd really made the clean getaway she planned. "That'd be nice, wouldn't it?"

"Has this guy threatened you, Mary?" His voice was low and sharp. Mac's eyes darkened to an intense glare as he sat back against the wall, his long legs extended across the narrow stairway. He'd formed a barrier between her and the door, protective, even though she was sure he hadn't consciously done so.

"Thornton threatens everybody. He's one of those

people who's a powerful friend but a more powerful enemy. But if you mean has he threatened me personally, physically, no. Again, that'd be too blunt for Thornton. That," she said, pointing to the check, "is his way of letting me know that he knows where I am." She tried to say it calmly, but it came out as the menace it was.

Mac was surprised at the worry in her eyes. She had an unsteady quality to her voice she probably thought she was hiding, but her body language was bordering on fear. "I think I get it now. You'd hoped to hide from this guy. Escape from the old Mary and her job out here in the middle of nowhere. Well, it explains a lot." He paused for a moment. "I'm not sure it's any of my business, but you look anything but calm. Are things more…personal than that between you and your old boss?"

"No. Well, he took my leaving very personally, but it's not like you think. It's just that no one walks out on Thornton Maxwell. He'd fire anyone in a heartbeat, but you don't quit until he tells you to. He doesn't want me back because he wants me, he wants me back because that way he wins." She poked at the offending check with a cautious finger. "And Thornton will do just about anything to win."

"If this guy worries you so much, don't you think maybe you need to talk to the police?"

She forced out a tight laugh. "Oh, that'd do wonders for my entrance into the community, don't you think? 'New drama director reveals own stalker.' Harbinger of the Bippo Bear boogeyman—that's just the first impression I'd want to make."

"You didn't choose this. People here wouldn't hold that against you." He tried to crack a joke to ease the tension.

"As for the bear song, I can't make promises, but no one in Middleburg would hold a jerk like Thornton against you."

"He'd never come here." It was the most unconvincing statement Mac had ever heard. She didn't believe that—not for a second—and it came through in every word.

He moved a few inches closer to her on the stairs. "Mary," he said, making his voice as gentle as he knew how, "would he hurt you?"

"No," she replied far too quickly. When his gaze held her eyes for a moment, she said "Not really." She broke away from his gaze and looked down. "I don't know."

That made Mac's stomach ignite. "Over a job? Over stuffed bears? What kind of a monster is this guy?"

"His job is his life. The Bippo Bear account was his personal coup, and he thinks he needs me to keep it. I just figured he'd move onto his next protégé when he got tired of me. But then the campaigns became successful, and Thornton likes success enough to make very sure he stays successful. He told me I could never leave, never work for anyone else but him, and like I said, you don't 'just say no' to Thornton Maxwell."

Watch me, Mac thought. It struck him, as she pulled her knees up to hug them to her chest, that it made perfect sense now why she'd want to surround herself with people on Christmas Eve. If Thornton hadn't actually threatened her physically, he'd come mighty close. And maybe it wasn't even a conscious thought to her, maybe she really did think the potluck was a path to town unity and her fears just made the idea that more appealing. "Has he sent you anything threatening? A bear full of razor blades or something?"

"No."

"That's your money, right? You earned it?"

"Yes."

"Then cash the check. There have to be ways to get yourself over this." She needed to get into the community, get a jump start on this new life she seemed eager to build. "Like coming to Gil and Emily's on Friday night. It's going to be the Christmas party to end all Christmas parties, and you'll be surrounded by people."

"Emily's already invited me, but…"

"But nothing. You need to go. I'll even take you out there myself. Seems to me, the best defense you have against your old life is to get on with your new life and be happy."

She looked unconvinced. "I don't know." She stood up and gathered the pile of mail.

"You don't have to know," he declared, deciding not to take no for an answer. "I know. I'll pick you up at 6:30. If you own a Christmas sweater, this is the place to trot it out. You have to wear red or green or you don't get in. *Really.*"

Chapter Ten

At the sound of Mac's engine, Gil came out of the barn coiling a length of rope and grinning. "Mr. Mayor. Nice of you to drop on by. I had something to ask you after rehearsal tonight, but you beat me to the punch. What's up?"

Mac cut the engine and walked toward the barn. "A few developments you ought to know about."

"Sounds intriguing." He nodded toward the tack room in the barn, where a pair of wooden chairs sat propped up against the wall. He flicked on the lights and the little space heater, then hung the rope up on a peg, and sat down. "Let's hear it."

"Well, you know Mary Thorpe used to live in Chicago," Mac began as he sat down. "It seems her previous boss wasn't too keen on seeing her go and might be applying a lot of pressure. She's a bit of a surprise, our Mary."

"Good thing you can be there for her." Gil grinned. A wide teasing grin.

"Hey, cut that out."

"I'm just saying you always seem to be around at the right moment. You might think God set it up or something." Gil sat back in his chair and folded his hands behind his head in frustrating confidence. "So you like her and you want to make sure she's okay. That's a good thing. Civic, even." He brought his hands back down and looked at Mac. "You do like her, don't you?"

"Depends on who you ask. If you talk to Ma, we're all but ring shopping." Mac threw his hands up in exasperation. "Come on, Gil, you live here, you know the rumor mill. It's impossible to see someone 'casually' in this town. Middleburg makes a couple go from zero to serious in under six seconds. And I'm not ready for serious. Not with her."

"You just told me all the reasons why you *shouldn't* like her, but that ain't answering my question, is it?"

"She's nice." Mac wanted to whack his forehead for not being able to come up with anything more convincing than that. Gil's expression told him "nice" had definitely not been convincing. "But that's all." Like that helped.

Truth was, he found her more than nice. But that was the trouble with small towns, there was no way to stay at "nice." If he was found "out" with her alone again, the snowball of predictions and gossip would begin rolling and there'd be more drama than any campaign could ever generate. Mac knew all these reasonable objections, he could recite them on command, but it hadn't stopped him from looking up at his office ceiling instead of working for many days now.

He'd bought a jazz violin CD when he was in a bookstore in Lexington the other day—a jazz violin CD—just because they'd been playing it over the store sound system and it sounded like her. Worse yet, he'd opened it and popped it into the car stereo before he even got home.

"Forget the rumor mill," Gil advised. "You think I

haven't known you long enough to pick up on it? Do you realize you've talked about her every time we've seen each other? You stare at her. It's kind of like the way you stare at a bridge that isn't working right, and that's kinda weird when you think about it, but you definitely stare. She gets to you. I think that's the only way you'd ever parade onstage in a blue bathrobe. Take a chance and bring her to the party Friday."

"Um…I already asked her." Talk about the worst idea ever. Why had he gone and asked her?

"She seems *very* nice," Gil conceded, still grinning. "A little more delicate that I would have picked for you, but it seems to bring out your hero tendencies. Snake-hunter. Actor. A regular renaissance mayor."

Mac launched off his chair to pace the small room. "You can be a real jerk sometimes, you know that, Sorrent?"

"Emily says so, especially when I'm right." He motioned for Mac to sit back down. "So she got to you. It was bound to happen sometime—why not now? You said you were feeling restless. Maybe it was more than just political unrest."

"*Why not now?* Because this is the worst time ever. She's not in the same place as me, faith-wise. And in the middle of this mayor thing? If I do bring Mary on Friday, it'll just encourage Ma. She's already more than a bit nutty about the thought of having a thirty-year-old still-bachelor son. She'd be all over this, knitting for grandbabies by Saturday morning."

"It's not like you've never dated before, Mac. You can handle your Ma and anyone else who jumps to conclusions. Bring her Friday." His grin made Mac want to throw him in a horse stall. Headfirst.

"I have to, now. That was the stupidest thing to do. Seriously."

Gil pulled a clipboard off the tack room wall and headed for the door. "Maybe not. You're always talking about how no one in Middleburg is willing to explore the possibilities."

Mac followed, glad to know this ridiculous conversation was coming to a close. "You *want* me to date her?"

"I want you to be happy. My baby deserves a happy godfather."

"Like you've ever really cared about…" Mac stopped. "*What* did you just say?"

Gil turned with the strangest look Mac had ever seen on his face. "I said my baby deserves a happy godfather. Mayor or not, no miserable man gets to godfather my baby."

Mac picked up his jaw off the floor. "Emily's *pregnant?*"

"She is indeed."

Gil was going to be a father. The guy he'd thrown into mud puddles in second grade was going to be a father. "You're gonna be a dad."

"It generally works that way, yes."

Mac grabbed his friend and pulled him into a quick hug. Gil and Emily were going to start a family. It was one of the best shocks he'd ever had. "Congratulations. Wow. When?"

"Sometime in June. We haven't told too many people yet. Emily's had a few complications and we thought it better to keep it private for a little while longer. The Mary role is a big deal for her, and now you know why. But you need to keep this under your hat for a while, especially on Friday. Consider it your first duty as godfather. You will, won't you?"

"Godfather? Of course. And sure, I'll keep quiet. But man, that's amazing news. Are you excited?"

Gil actually looked jittery, which was saying something on his usually stoic features. "Excited, freaked out, worried, amazed, running out of ways to cope with that herd of hormones putting up a Christmas tree in my kitchen...I'm all sorts of things. Just not sane."

His kitchen? Gil'd been married for how long and still thought of it as "his kitchen"? He could just imagine how well that was going. Gil had been surrounded by men—farmers, foremen, the teenagers and twenty-something men whose lives he had helped rebuild—just a little bit too long. Mac slapped Gil on the shoulder. "You've been raising great big kids for five years. How much harder can one tiny guy be?"

"*If* it's a guy." Gil practically gulped the sentiment.

The thought of what Gil's frilly, vintage-loving wife would do with a baby girl made Mac break into an amused grin. He imagined Gil holding a frothy bundle of pink lace in those great big farmer hands, and broke out laughing. "Now who's in more trouble? You or me?"

Pastor Dave came to Mary's office door early in the afternoon, as she was marking lighting cues on a script. The high school had lent the church two spotlights, both of which had a selection of color choices, so she had the chance to add a few small-scale special effects to her production. Now, when Mary and Joseph walked through the Bethlehem night, it could actually *look* like night onstage. Progress in inches, she thought. "Mary?" Pastor said as he knocked on the open door. He'd brought her a cup of coffee. People were always bringing each other coffee in this town.

"Oh, I could sure use that. Thanks." She rose and took the steaming mug, coming around her desk so they could sit on the pair of chairs in front. She had an office, with actual chairs, instead of her cubicle at the ad agency and her locker at the symphony hall. That felt so good.

"You're doing a great job. They can be an unruly bunch, even on their best days." He sighed. "Tonight, they may be at their worst."

Evidently the coffee was for fortification. "What's up?"

"I just got off the phone with Sandy Burnside. Evidently Mac and Howard got in a bit of a row at the dime store this afternoon. The store started offering a ten percent discount to Epson supporters. Which made the car wash across the street offer a ten percent discount to MacCarthy voters. Mac and Howard ended up shouting at each other with the store owners in the middle of the street until a policeman had to ask everyone to leave. Quite a row, evidently. They've been civil so far, but things are clearly getting out of hand." He shook his head. "I don't know what's gotten into folks."

Mary had visions of a cowboy saloon fight, with dusty buckaroos being thrown out swinging shutter doors by a star-studded sheriff. "Voting discounts? That's ridiculous."

"Once people start taking sides, it doesn't take much to get things out of hand." He set his coffee down. "They'll show up tonight, but they'll be prickly, that's for sure. You have your work cut out for you."

"Oh, boy," she murmured over a gulp of her coffee.

"It's tough." Dave nodded. "But this is *exactly* why you're here. Folks need a place to put aside their differences for a common goal." He rose from the chair. "You just hang onto the reins tonight, and don't let 'em start up again. Forewarned is forearmed."

"Well, tonight's the night they all have to have their lines memorized. Fortunately, that tends to put people in their place very quickly."

"You want me to come? Watch over things?"

While it was an attractive idea, Mary thought it best to hold onto what little ground she had. "Well, keep your cell phone on and I'll have you on my speed dial."

Pastor Dave laughed. "Pastoral 9-1-1? Good enough. Sandy'll be there, too, and Gil, and those two could wrangle just about anyone if you need backup."

"Sounds like I'll need every heavenly host I can get my hands on."

Mary did keep them in line, but only barely. The tension in the church hall was thick enough to cut with a hatchet, much less a knife. Howard said nothing all evening— except his lines of course, and bristled with annoyance and discomfort. Mostly he just frowned and made a point of sitting as physically far from Mac as possible.

Mac, on the other hand, was openly prickly. More than once she'd had to "shush" him from a cutting comment or other whispered comeback to something someone else said. She'd spent half the rehearsal wondering whether or not to follow the policeman's lead and just dismiss the two, but it was equally clear that dozens of other people would take up the argument in their absence. She pretended she hadn't heard about the fiasco, hoping a feigned ignorance would save her from having to take sides.

More spiritually mature, hm? Who'd say that based on how you just behaved tonight?

Mac hung back after rehearsal, recognizing how he'd behaved and wanting to apologize for the jerk he'd been this evening. Actually, he'd been a jerk most of the day. With the discount stunt, Mac felt like Howard's supporters were out to get him, and it was pretty clear Howard felt equally threatened. How had it eroded into this bickering? Mac didn't run to create scenes like this, and he doubted Howard found them useful, either. He did his best to put it behind him for the rehearsal, but he hadn't done a very good job.

Mary wasn't exactly scowling when she gathered up her coat, but she was close. "Are you two going to be able to get this under control?" she asked in a tone that was way too teacher-ish.

"I'm sorry," Mac said in a tone that was way too much like a third-grade ruffian. "Things got out of hand today."

"You can say that again. I'm glad Pastor Dave warned me, or I'd have been blindsided."

Great. Pastor Dave had found it necessary to warn her. It was the grown-up version of having the principal send a note home to your mother. He pushed the wave of annoyance back down into his gut and deliberately unclenched his fists as he pulled open the church door for her. "You didn't deserve to get pulled into this."

She looked at him. "Actually, when you think about it, maybe I did. I'm supposed to be the distraction from all that. It'd be foolish to think it wouldn't find its way into rehearsal now and then. It's actually kind of amusing, from where I sit anyway. Discounts. You all are acting like children. Stomping and snorting around each other like angry bulls."

"No cow metaphors, please, this is horse country."

She laughed. "Actually, when Pastor Dave told me the police broke up your fighting in the street, that's just what I pictured. The whole cowboy-burst-through-the-swinging-doors-of-the-saloon thing. So is that a cow metaphor, or a horse metaphor?"

That made him laugh. "That question doesn't even merit an answer." The western-movie vision hit him anyway: him standing in a dusty alley, hand twitching over his holster, ready to shoot it out with Howard at the O.K. Corral. He laughed harder.

"That's better." She pulled on her gloves and they walked in silence past the huge lit Christmas tree in the park. After a pause, she asked "Is it worth it? All this bickering?"

"You mean am I sorry I ran? No." He tucked his own hands into his pockets; the evening had turned cold and damp. "I'm sorry it gets messy like that, but this is a small town and people are all up in each other's business all the time here. If we cut out just because we argued, we'd never do anything. Howard and I will be fine after this is over." He turned to look at her. "Maybe not *right* after all this is over, but fine eventually."

"I find that hard to believe. Isn't this the part of the country where families feud for generations? Hatfields and McCoys and all that?"

"Oh, please. A woman as smart as you should know better than to buy into a stereotype like that. Short of the occasional 'y'all,' have you seen anything that would make you believe that?"

A wry grin crept across her face. "Were you in the same church I was tonight?"

"Okay, above and beyond the normal human bickering factor."

The grin didn't let up. She was sparring with him, and he was enjoying it. "Is there a normal human bickering factor?"

Mac shrugged deeper into his coat, pretending at an annoyance he no longer felt. "I thought we were discussing my call to civil service."

She mimicked his formality, the grin now a full-fledged smile. "Oh, yes, of course. Expound, please."

That made him raise an eyebrow. "Expound? Quite a 'hundred-dollar word' as Sandy would say."

"I do have an advanced education. I'm only two years and a eighty-page thesis away from a doctorate."

He chuckled. "And you write jingles. *Wrote* jingles. Or will you continue to sell blue bears on the side? I doubt the Christmas Drama Coordinator pays much of a living wage."

Now she played at annoyance. It satisfied him, on some level, that they'd reached the ability to joke—even lightly—about Bippo Bears. His dad always said you never really conquered something until you could laugh at it. "I believe we were discussing your call to civil service."

He nodded. "And I can't miss my chance to expound now, can I?" They stopped to admire a shop window done up for the holiday, all full of snow globes and an elegant crèche.

"Howard's missing the point on too many things. Things that are going to be crucial for Middleburg in the next couple of years. We need more compromises if we're going to survive. Howard thinks the way to stay charming and quaint is to make sure nothing changes. I think Middleburg can keep what makes it Middleburg and still walk into the future. It's 'change or die' these days, and I don't want to see my town die. A change of mayor, or even just the *idea* of a choice of mayor, is a good place to start." He shrugged his shoulders, aware that he'd given her quite a speech. "I'll get off my soapbox now," he said, motioning for them to continue walking. "But I've got a question for you first."

Chapter Eleven

Mary wasn't sure what question Mac had in mind. "Okay," she said a bit warily. She made herself promise to answer, even if it felt like tiptoeing out onto thin ice.

"Why are you alone at Christmas? I know you have parents and a brother and his wife, you must have had other places you could have gone for the holidays than to come here where you didn't know anyone."

She felt her spine straighten, her defenses rise. "What makes you think I'll be alone at Christmas?"

"I don't think you'd be pushing so hard for the potluck if you had somewhere else to be."

Her first thought was that he was shooting holes in her reasoning, knocking down her plan to get the town together on Christmas Eve. When she looked at him, however, she realized it was a genuine question.

Tell him, she told herself. It's no secret. Still, it felt like she was letting out private information she wasn't quite ready to share. "My parents were planning to come at first. But my brother hasn't been well. They called just after I took this job and asked if it would be okay with me if they spent the holidays with my brother since he needs the help. They invited me to come out, offered to pay my plane ticket to fly in on Christmas Day even though I can afford my own airfare. I almost did, but then it just seemed to me that maybe here was the best place for me to be after all."

"Why?"

Mary wasn't sure she was ready to get into this with him. He wasn't prying, he just didn't realize how personal a question that was. "It's complicated," she answered, just to buy herself a moment to think. "I haven't been a Christian for very long. I mean I always believed, my parents took me to church every once in a while, but it was never anything real. Anything personal or meaningful. When you work in retail advertising and in music, Christmas is crunch season. You're working long hours, and almost every working musician I know has a job on Christmas Eve or Christmas Day if not both. 'Christmas is a music holiday, but it's not a holiday for musicians,' my college professor would say."

"I suppose you're right," Mac said thoughtfully. "Never thought about it that way before, but it's true."

"Last Christmas, it just struck me how empty it all was. The sales figures, the concerts, the drinking and hard partying. It was like we were all going out of our way to have fun just to convince ourselves we weren't missing out on anything. Thornton used to proclaim 'We make Christmas.' Last year I realized I didn't want to make Christmas, I wanted to *have* Christmas. Or what was *behind* Christmas."

"Meaning Christ?"

"Yeah, although I didn't know it at first. It was like I was gravitating toward church, being pulled in to places and people who seemed to have whatever it was that was supposed to be behind Christmas. And when it all finally clicked, when it fell into place and I realized that I needed Christ, needed that faith, then everything I did before seemed so…pointless. Hollow." She allowed herself to look at him, to gauge whether or not her poor explanation was making any sense. "I'm not very good at explaining it."

"No," he responded more warmly than she would have expected. Certainly more warmly than her parents had reacted. "I get it," he agreed. "You didn't need just a minor alteration, you needed a clean break, a major overhaul. To go somewhere completely new and different. I get that."

"I'm glad somebody does." She tried to laugh, but it didn't quite work.

"I take it your mom and dad aren't exactly thrilled with your choice?"

"They paid a lot of money for my education. This feels like a huge step backward for them, and they don't understand why I'm leaving a lucrative career for a 'Podunk part-time job.'"

They'd reached his office and her apartment, and she found herself sorry this conversation had to end just when it had gotten started. It felt enormously satisfying to find someone else who understood why she'd turned her life upside down.

He stood in the doorway while she got out her keys. "Faith rarely makes sense to folks who don't have it. If you haven't figured that out yet, you will. God asks us to do things that don't follow logic."

"Like an unheard-of campaign for mayor?"

"Yeah." He laughed. "Just like that." He stuffed his hands in his pockets and took a step back as her key turned the lock. "You keep at it, Mary Thorpe. Middleburg's a good place to launch a fresh start. You might do okay here."

"You think?"

There was a look in his eye, a split second of carefully guarded affection, that tripped up her pulse before she could reason it away.

"Yeah," he said. "I think. Don't let that fool Thornton take that away."

The mention of Thornton's name sucked the warmth out of the air. It struck her that she was going upstairs to an empty apartment, and for a moment she felt the urge to ask Mac to stay and talk awhile. Which was a really bad idea. Before she could stop herself, she heard herself ask, "We're going Friday to Gil and Emily's, right?"

"Sure." Mac smiled, nodded and hit some button on his key chain that turned on his zippy orange sports car without him even being inside the thing. He smirked as behind him in the parking space outside his office, the coupe's lights and engine roared to life.

"You're a show-off," she teased him.

"Guilty," he said as he turned and opened the car door. "Curly had to learn it somewhere."

Friday night, Mac was nervous. Actually nervous. He couldn't remember the last time he'd felt nervous about a woman, which made it worse. He felt an attraction to her, true, but also wanted to protect her from the small-town talk that would surely be the result of their appearance tonight. Even though the threat of gossip wouldn't have bugged him before, he felt differently about subjecting Mary to any of it. He wanted tonight to be about all the good things a small town could be. To give her a shred of that old-fashioned Christmas she seemed to want so badly.

After all, she was new to her faith and this Christmas would be special for her. Mac had to tread carefully, though. If she was so drawn to old-fashioned charm, she was probably the kind of woman eager to settle down— and he was not that kind of man. And this was feeling a little too much like that kind of date.

She was buttoning up her jacket as she came down the stairs, and he caught a glimpse of her pale neck above a mint-green sweater. The sweater was the fuzzy kind, with little silver sparkles woven into it. It looked elegant, but festive, and it made the creamy-white-blonde of her hair nearly glow. She'd put on lipstick and wore little sparkly snowflake earrings that kept absconding with his attention even when he tried to look elsewhere.

She caught him looking at her and blushed. "You said we had to wear red or green. This was the closest thing to Christmas green I had."

"It's fine," he said earnestly. She did look fine, very fine. He opened the car door and let her step in.

"What do you think?" he asked as he slid into the driver's seat. Even parked, a Nissan 350Z was an impressive little roadster, and he knew it.

She grinned. "Very snazzy. It suits you. You don't strike me as the truck type, anyway."

"Oh, I own one, back at the house. For yard stuff and all." He patted the dash of the two-seater convertible with admiration. "You'd never catch me loading bags of mulch into this baby."

She laughed and looked around. "They wouldn't fit anyway."

"It's more fun with the top down, but we'd freeze."

"I'll wait till spring, thanks."

They made small talk for the short drive out to Gil's farm, commenting on the blanket of Christmas lights Emily had set up outside. He'd seen the inside yesterday, and it rivaled a department store window. Emily had claimed she wasn't half done, and it already had twice the decorations he'd seen on any other home. It was going to be fun watching Mary take it all in.

It was. "Wow," she noted, accepting a cup of spiced cider after they'd done a quick tour of the house. "Gil wasn't kidding."

Mac could barely contain his laughter when Gil, man of the daily flannel shirt, appeared in a red striped sweater. Sure he couldn't say anything without cracking up, Mac just gave Gil a sharp look and a nod, to which Gil raised an eyebrow that broadcast, "You wanna make something of it?" The image of Gil making goo-goo faces at an infant invaded his brain with a shock. Gil's going to be a father. *The world is shifting, Lord.*

"Emily's gone bananas," Gil muttered. "Each horse has its own wreath up on the stalls. She gave the guys Santa hats to wear, but they refused. The horses have their own tree, for crying out loud."

"This I gotta see," Mac declared, nodding in the direction of the barn behind the house. "Want to come?"

"You two go," Gil declined. "I'd best stay with Emily before she starts hanging mistletoe everywhere. That woman's dangerous in her condition."

Mary laughed and without thinking, Mac took her hand and led her to the back door, where he grabbed a thick red blanket off a bench and wrapped it around her as they dashed across the yard to the horse barn.

"Oh, my," Mary observed, pulling the blanket closer as they walked down the aisle separating the horse stalls in

Gil's barn. Sure enough, each stall had its own wreath, and each wreath had the horse's name spelled out in glitter on a red velvet bow. "He wasn't kidding."

Mac couldn't help but laugh. Gil must be reaching the edge of his endurance with all of Emily's decorations. "That woman takes 'deck the halls' a bit too seriously."

Mary touched one of the wreaths. "Romeo. Lady Macbeth. All the horses have names from Shakespeare."

"Yep. For all his rough exterior, Gil's a well-educated guy. Both book smarts and the school of hard knocks. I'm glad to see him so happy."

"They are, aren't they? Emily's so excited to be expecting."

"I'm the godfather, you know. Gil asked me the other day." He was busting-his-buttons proud but since they hadn't revealed the pregnancy to anyone, he'd had to keep it to himself. She knew, though, so he was glad to be able to talk about it to someone.

"In deference to your humble spirit, no doubt," she teased, her blue eyes glinting under that fringe of bangs. "Or is it to curry political favor with the next mayor of Middleburg?"

"'Curry favor'?" He gave her a challenging look. "Let's put those hundred-dollar city words of yours on a horse for ten minutes and see how well you ride." He broadened his Kentucky twang and swaggered over to her. "Don't pick a fight with a horseman in a barn unlessen you can hold your own."

"It just so happens that I can ride horses. Just the kind that go up and down on poles, that's all. I have also ridden lions and unicorns, for that matter."

There it was again. A glimpse of that amazing spunk. What had beaten the fight out of her in Chicago? He looked at her, his engineering mind trying to solve the logical puzzle of her but getting lost in the definitely illogical allure of her eyes. The way she tucked her hair behind her ears. He wondered if that freshness, that sense of newness in her expression, was there for him when he first came to faith. It seemed almost too long ago to remember, even though it had been just under a decade. She struck him as both jaded and innocent—another illogical impression. She was a paradox, which is a very dangerous and irresistible thing to throw at an engineer.

Suddenly—and then again, maybe not so suddenly—alone in the barn seemed a dangerous and irresistible place to be with her. Mac felt them teetering on the edge of a place where they shouldn't go.

She must have felt it, too, for Mary shivered and declared, "We should get back. It's freezing out here."

They wandered in and out of the party, sometimes moving through the large farmhouse's many rooms together, other times being swept into different conversational groups. He kept "half an eye" on her as Pa always said, half listening for her voice or occasionally glancing her way to see where she was when they weren't together. Just as he expected, people were welcoming Mary warmly; she got the stuffing hugged out of her from Sandy Burnside, and Emily pulled her all around the room making introductions to any Middleburgian she hadn't yet met. He caught Mary laughing uproariously in the kitchen with Dinah and Janet one minute, and getting a demonstration of Gil's monstrous flat-screen television from one of the farm's teenage boys the next. She was fitting in just fine, looking more comfortable as the evening went on. As he took to the piano the way he always did at parties, even

Howard pulled her into a song or two with no hint of the tension everyone had seen at rehearsal. For a split second, he thought he should have asked Mary to bring her violin, remembering the jazzy number he'd heard in the choir loft. She could probably pick up a bit of bluegrass twang with little or no effort and be a hit in no time.

Things seemed to be going wonderfully until the same teen burst into the living room with the television remote still in his hand. "Mr. Gil," he interrupted far too loudly, "you gotta see this. These people are nuts!"

Like everyone else within earshot, Mac followed Gil and the crowd into the den. And gulped.

There, in high-definition clarity, was a live news shot of a knockdown, drag-out fight taking place at a nearby mall. Something close to a riot had broken out at a discount chain store, and the cameras were getting spectacular shots of one man throwing punches at another man. A man who protected a Bippo Bear box behind his back. "Bippo Bear Brawl" flashed under the shot as the camera cut to a disgusted-looking newswoman. "'Tis the season," she began singing in the Bippo Bear melody, "to misbehave, even if Santa is watching." Mac silently berated the television as he scanned the crowd for Mary. "The mad craze to get Bippo Bears took a turn for the worse today," the newswoman went on, "as two men let the stress of the holiday and the craving for those stuffed blue bears get the better of them...."

She continued, but Mac didn't hear the rest of it. He darted through the crowd gathering in Gil's den, hoping to head off Mary before she caught a glimpse of this. The brawl might serve as conversation, entertainment even, for the rest of the partygoers, but it would hurt Mary to the core.

He was too late. Just as he cleared the edge of the crowd, he saw her, standing in the hallway with a clear shot at the television, her face a mix of horror and guilt. Speeding up his steps, he caught her elbow and tried to drag her out of the den as the camera showed a close-up of the two grown men hurling insults and actual punches at each other. It was like one of those ridiculous tabloid talk shows, only it was happening less than twenty miles from where they stood. "C'mon, Mary, you don't need to see this."

"See this?" she whispered harshly, "I *did* this. Did you hear her? She was singing my song."

"There's no point in watching this." This was the excruciating moment when the crowd in the den began talking among themselves about the evils of Christmas toy marketing. He had to get her out of here—which wouldn't be hard, because she looked like she was going to bolt any minute.

"It's an abomination," Howard asserted as his voice rose above the rest while Mac pulled Mary through the hall toward the other end of the house. "Don't those toy people know better?"

"Don't those grown men know better?" came Sandy's voice in reply. "What fools put this nonsense on the television anyway?"

"Mary…" Mac began, not even sure what to say.

"Don't!" She objected sharply, putting her forehead against the hallway wall. "Don't even try to make this better. I knew I couldn't run from this. I knew I'd have to pay for what I'd done."

Mac started to say something about taking the drama a bit too far, but he bit back his comment. "You didn't do that," he argued, even though he doubted it would have any effect.

"Didn't I? My directives were to create a song kids could bug their parents with. To drive parents to the kind of shopping frenzy we just saw." She glared at him. "How can you say I didn't do that? I did *just* that."

Months of worry, and stress she hadn't even realized had built up, boiled over into an unreasonable panic that grabbed hold of Mary and wouldn't let go. "I'm sorry I ever did any of it," Mary blurted out for the hundredth time.

Mac shifted his weight. "Don't you think you're taking this a bit far?"

Easy for him to say. Mary flung one hand in the direction of the talking behind them. "People—parents—are behaving like animals and I started the feeding frenzy. They'll hate me once they know." The world worked the same everywhere. You were only as good—or as bad—as your latest accomplishment. This news would overshadow whatever brief history she'd had with these people, and parents were likely to run her out of town once they knew.

"I know. I don't hate you. The question is, do *you* hate you?"

What a pointless question. She simply scowled at him. This was not the kind of situation that could be placated by a simple "Jesus loves you." Actions—*consequences*—mattered.

"Did you tell them to behave like that? Does it say 'hit each other' anywhere in that song?"

"Don't oversimplify this. It was my job to 'create the craving' as Thornton always put it. I did my job exceptionally well, don't you think? I really should get an award for this one."

"I've got a thing for Dinah's snickerdoodles. She intentionally leaves the bakery door open when she bakes them because the smell is so good. And I get it full force, right next door. When I smell those cookies, I want 'em. Bad. But it wouldn't be Dinah's fault if I held up the bakery to get them."

"It's not the same." Why was he trying to reason with her?

"Of course it's the same. You just won't see it that way. Look, Howard's a good fifty pounds overweight, mostly thanks to Gina Deacon's pies. He knows it, Gina knows it. Howard doesn't hate Gina. As a matter of fact, he's mighty fond of her. They've been friends for twenty-five years." Mac leaned up along the wall beside her. "I know you feel bad about what you did, but feeling bad isn't the same thing as being guilty. You're not guilty of anything. In fact, you did something most people wouldn't have had the nerve to do—you walked away from all that. You've got this blown way out of proportion in your head. The only person who thinks Bippo Bears are your crime is *you.*"

"You don't know that."

That got his dander up. "No, I *do* know that. You think this is such a black mark on you. Haven't you figured it out yet, Mary? Every one of us has got a black mark." Now it was his turn to glare at her. "It's the whole point of Christmas. Bippo Bears weren't the first Christmas craze, and they won't be the last. So how about you use all your talents—the ones you think have been so bad—to focus people on the real point of Christmas. You're doing it. You're proving to be just as good at this job as you were at the other one. People won't stop liking you if they know. Why can't you see that?"

He was Middleburg's favorite son, running for mayor, for crying out loud. A model citizen even if he did have a touch of the renegade in him. "And how on earth would you know?"

Chapter Twelve

He didn't know. Mary was right. He wouldn't know if Middleburg was as forgiving as he said because he hadn't given them the chance to forgive his big black mark, either. That's why he couldn't sleep. He'd figured out why Mary's predicament seemed to bother him so much. Some part of him had known for months that his "senior prank" had to come to light, he just kept convincing himself it no longer mattered.

It mattered. Now that he was running for mayor, against Howard, it mattered more than ever.

And it mattered because he couldn't tell Mary one thing while he was doing just the opposite. She'd asked that he take her home almost immediately after the fiasco, saying she didn't feel well. It didn't help that everyone seemed to think they were just trying to steal a moment alone. Every time he dismissed her fear as illogical and out of proportion, his own came barreling back to him. God's final blow came when he opened his Bible for guidance and found himself smack at the verse about "the log in your own eye."

How dare he judge her for thinking her secret loomed

so gigantic and harmful that she couldn't bear the thought of telling people? Hadn't he done just the same? He'd managed to dismiss it over the years as the unfortunate centerpiece of a large collection of high school pranks—some less harmless than others, dismissing it as a "small sin." But it wasn't small, it wasn't harmless, and if he really was the kind of man who could lead Middleburg, he needed to be the kind of man who could own up to this.

And not just for him. Mac couldn't sit there and assure Mary that Middleburg wouldn't lynch her for writing the Bippo Bear song if he believed Middleburg wouldn't forgive him for what he'd done.

God had made it abundantly clear that Mary Thorpe needed to hear his secret. From him. And it couldn't stop there: Howard and all of Middleburg would have to hear it from him, as well.

I hate this character-building business, Lord, Mac complained as he wandered the church looking for her the next afternoon. *You ask such hard things.* He had to walk past the manger setting, bearing the quiet message of all the hard things God had asked of His Son, and felt his throat constrict.

He found her in the back of the sanctuary, fumbling with a very industrial-looking key chain. "Just the guy I need," she said, trying to sound natural even though there was tension between them. "I need to see if there's a prop stored upstairs. Pastor Dave said there was a huge star used in a Christmas concert a couple of years back, and he thinks it's still all the way up in the steeple."

The steeple. God had cornered him, and he knew it. For the first time since high school, Mac felt his palms sweat.

"I've never been up in a steeple before," she continued

as they started up the church stairs toward the choir loft where the hatchway to the steeple was.

"It's not very exciting," Mac stated, thinking his voice had gone up six notes from the tension. "It's not like it has windows and you can see out over the town or anything."

"You've been up there before?"

He didn't want to answer that. "I've been all over every corner of this church. When I was in the seventh grade, our youth pastor's favorite game was something called 'Sardines.'"

"Oh, I've played that. Sort of like Hide and Seek, isn't it?"

"Yeah, only more troublesome." He gestured for her to go first up the steep narrow stairway to the choir loft. He noticed, as she passed him, that her hair smelled good. He felt the hair on the back of his neck stand on end, and tried to casually wipe his palms on his pant legs as he started up the stairs behind her.

His memory of that night in the steeple loomed like a grown-up monster in the closet. As much as he didn't want to tell her about it, he knew that if he didn't, this feeling would only get worse. When she wrestled the padlock off the small hatch door, he went first, like diving into a cold lake to get the shock over with fast.

He thought it would be cold. It was December after all, and this corner of the church wasn't heated. But as an engineer, he also knew heat rose, and as one of the highest points of the church, it had collected sufficient heat to feel comfortable if not cozy. The sharp angles of the steeple formed a little cone-shaped room, dusty and dark until he reached for the cord that he knew turned on the single bare light bulb hung from the ceiling. She came up behind him, wide-eyed, turning in a small circle to take in the room.

"I used to imagine secret rooms like this," she revealed in a hushed tone that tickled down his spine. "Chicago apartments are just white-walled boxes. I always wanted a top-of-the-tower secret room like this in my building."

He found the space unattractive at the moment, but hearing her voice, Mac could remember his own fascination with it when he was younger. He'd been caught up here dozens of times—sometimes getting into trouble, sometimes just being alone when everyone else was in choir practice or church banquets or whatever.

Mary begin rummaging through bins and boxes. "It's a pretty big star, it shouldn't be too hard to find."

In truth, the thing was right behind her, she just hadn't seen it. "Like that?" Managing a grin, he pointed, and she spun around to see a large silver star shape covered in shiny tin.

"That's it." She moved aside a few rolls of what looked like old wallpaper and pulled out the star. While the top was intact, the bottom point was in fact completely snapped off. It looked more like an awkward silver crown than any kind of celestial beacon. "Oh, I suppose this won't do after all." She gave a little sigh. "We can build a new one." She put the leftover star back down and then turned to sit on a wooden box. "It was still fun to discover this place."

God had pretty much handed Mac his opening. He sat down on a box across from her—although with nowhere near as much grace. The roof's sharp angles made it difficult for someone of his height to move easily. Had he really been that much shorter in high school? "Yeah," he concurred, pulling up his knees to rest his elbows on them. "I had a little too much fun up here in high school."

That brought out a scandalous look from her. "Little Joey MacCarthy stealing kisses in the church steeple?"

For a split second he thought that the perfect lie. He could just say yes, they'd laugh about the recklessness of youth and it'd be over. But it wouldn't be over. "I got into a bit more trouble than that," he began. "Mary…um… God's made it clear to me that there's something I should tell you." He shook his head, rolling his eyes. "Man, that sounds so incredibly stupid."

She looked puzzled, but she didn't say anything.

"I told you the folks in Middleburg will be all fine with your Bippo Bear thing. And they will, really. Even if twelve more fights break out in malls between now and Christmas."

She wasn't getting the connection, but then again why should she until he told her the story? "Believe it or not, I understand why you couldn't get out of Friday's party fast enough. I get it about having something you think makes you awful. Having a secret, something you're sure will brand you as the bad guy. I know yours. God seems to think you need to know mine."

"'God seems to think'?" she echoed, "What do you mean?"

"I sat there Friday night and told you that you were un-reasonable about the Bippo Bear thing. And I realized—or actually, God hounded it into me—that it's not fair to tell you that, if I can't pull that off myself. Truth is, you didn't bring me up here by accident." He ran his hands through his hair, feeling unbelievably awkward. A minute ago this felt important and painful, now it just felt ugly and ridiculous. "I'm not making a good start at this, am I?"

"Keep going…I'm confused, but I'll hang on. Although, I have to say, I didn't hear God making any commands to get you in the steeple."

"God doesn't always do the burning bush thing. Sometimes, like you said, He just lines up events in a way that you know He was working. So, even when it feels dumb…which would be now, by the way…you learn to go with it." Did he really just say that? His tongue was tangled worse than his brain.

She looked around, shrugged her shoulders and offered a small smile. "So, we're here in the steeple. Go with it."

"I've lived here my whole life, you know that. And kids do stupid things in high school, even if they grow up to run for mayor." He picked up an old, dusty candlestick and began fiddling with it. "I, well, I was a high-achiever in the stupid-kid stuff. If a prank happened at Middleburg High, it was a good guess that I was involved. Mostly dumb, harmless things. Toilet papering people's houses, letting animals out of barns, flying things from flagpoles, the kind of thing Pastor Dave would call 'shenanigans.'"

"I have heard a story or two," she offered. "Mostly from your mother."

"Yeah, well, like most mothers, she only knows the half of it." He put the candlestick down. "There was one thing I did—one pretty bad thing—that no one knows about. I mean everyone knows it happened, but no one knows I did it. I think it's part of why I ran for mayor, because I needed to prove that I was better than that stupid kid now."

She brushed a blond lock off her forehead. "I guess I follow you. You're saying that telling me to stop feeling guilty about the Bippo Bear song showed you that you've never come clean about…whatever it is you did?"

It sounded so logical the way she explained it. It had mostly just bumped around in his conscience until he couldn't stand it anymore. "Yeah, I suppose that's a good way to put it."

"That doesn't make a whole lot of sense."

"I know that. Believe me, I've talked myself out of this half a dozen times, but God doesn't seem to think I get to rest until I do this." He shot her a miserable look. He was used to having the witty remark, the perfect one-liner to gloss over the tense situation, and at the moment he was a babbling fool.

"Does it have to do with this steeple?" she guessed, reaching out and touching one of the dusty beams. She was trying to help, and that only made it worse.

"Actually, it does." He was mature enough in his faith that he should not be choking on this. He should understand the concept of forgiveness, should be man enough to own up to his own mistakes. But, like her irrational fear of what folks would think of Bippo Bears, sense never did seem to enter the picture on these things. Just start, he told himself. Just tell the story. "They were building the steeple, well, building this *new* one, back when I was a senior. The old church had a small steeple, and a few years back— before they built the preschool wing and all that stuff that got hurt in the storm that brought Drew here." He was digressing, avoiding the subject. He grunted, pulling his hands down across his face, frustrated with his own ridiculous weakness when it came to this. "I'd had a huge fight with a teacher. A math teacher that told me I'd never be an engineer if I couldn't get my Algebra grade up. I knew I wanted to be an engineer then, and it just seemed to me like this guy had it out for me, that he was purposely failing me. You know the way teenagers think, all doom and drama."

"I remember high school," she said, encouraging him with her eyes.

"I didn't exactly have the longest fuse back then, and I

stormed out of school. I came here to watch the construction, to prove to myself I could understand all of what they were doing. I tried to get them to let me help, but I was just a kid, and all the construction workers naturally wouldn't let me lend a hand, which just made me more angry. So I came back that night and climbed up the scaffolding into the steeple. It was May, and pretty warm, so I could sit up in the studs of it and look out over the town because the walls hadn't gone up yet."

He'd never told another living soul the next part. It felt like he had to drag the words out from somewhere deep in his gut. "I wanted to show everyone. And I got an idea. A horrible, mean, destructive idea. I'd never done anything like it before then or since. I wouldn't have even thought myself capable of something like it. But I found a hacksaw lying on the floor, and something came over me." Mac looked down, preferring not to meet her eyes. "I sawed through the studs, leaving just a bit of the wood, so that the first good wind would topple the steeple over. I didn't think about the people who could have gotten hurt or the damage that could have been done. I didn't think at all. It was a streak of mean. Pure mean. You know, I actually remember laughing when I did it. It was the worst thing. I can't even believe I was that kid. But I was."

He stopped for a moment, feeling the sensation of the secret leaving him. It was an odd combination—the lightness of release, the press of panic. He felt raw, almost wanting to wince from the feeling of being exposed, even to *one person*. How could she not be frightened of exposing herself to a *whole* town? "I hid the saw and snuck away, proud of my 'senior prank.' I went home and sat smugly in my bed, thinking I'd shown them all. I had great visions of the steeple smashing down into the church parking lot, sort of like my own private disaster movie playing in my head."

"What happened then?"

"Well, I was no idiot, and it turns out I may have botched Algebra but I knew my engineering geometry. I'd sawed in all the right places. I think I'd convinced myself that it couldn't really happen. That I'd just make the builders mad, slow them down, make them do the steeple over. But a storm did come in early the next morning. I'd picked all the right places to weaken, and the steeple came clear down off the roof. Howard had carpooled with the pastor to some weekend church function so his car was in the parking lot overnight. A large part of the steeple landed right on top of his car. The wood had smashed into enough pieces—and I'd sawed at enough odd angles—that no one ever saw the cuts I'd made. The congregation all assumed God had saved them from some horrible accident by showing them a weakness in the steeple before it was finished."

He stopped, letting the words evaporate into the air. It was out. Mac felt an excruciating tangle of emotions. "No one ever knew it was me. And I've never told anyone." For an awful second, some part of him panicked; a gut instinct of "she knows; she can expose me" that for all its irrationality felt chokingly real. He stole a glance at her, suddenly needing to know what she'd do now. *She knows.* It was thumping through his head like a pounding pulse. *She knows.* He knew that all his platitudes back at the farmhouse about how she shouldn't worry about people knowing were just that—useless phrases that belonged to logical thinking. And fear wasn't ever about logical thinking. *Why doesn't she say something?* The seconds seemed to stretch out endlessly.

"You've never told anyone you did this?"

It made him sound like such a moral weakling the way she said it. And that was half of the torment—not only was he owning up to the deed, but his weak inability to come forward. This was the crown jewel of "you should know better." If this was bad, what would it feel like to tell the whole town?

"You?" she said with the most awful look on her face. "You don't strike me as the kind. At least not now."

"Yeah, well, we all grow up, don't we?" The excuse he'd told himself for years now sounded worse than hollow.

"Don't you think…" she mentioned as she furrowed her eyebrows, calculating the time that had passed "…twelve years is enough time to let it all blow over? You're not fool enough to think people will hold this against you—now?" She realized her own words, echoing her fears that people would hold the Bippo Bear fiasco "against her," and an odd smile turned up one corner of her lips.

She had this enigmatic, Mona Lisa kind of smile. He felt the primal panic in his gut go down a notch or two. Some part of him knew she wouldn't brand him as a monster, but it was one of those things he had to actually see to believe. "I don't know," he responded, exhaling. "I'm dumb enough to run for mayor against Howard Epson."

Mary hugged her knees. "What do you think Howard will do when he finds out?" She didn't even have to say, "Because you are going to tell everyone now, aren't you?"

Mac had the sensation of being bound to her in an odd unspoken way, stuck together by their mutual secrets. *Is this what You were after, Lord? Putting us together like this? She frightens me. There, I said it. She makes me feel things I'm not ready for.*

"That dumb kid—the frustrated high school boy with the mean streak—are you still him inside?"

"Of course not," he shot back. Surprised at his harsh tone, he tried to crack a joke. "I'm still dumb and frustrated, but I've grown out of my mean streak." It fell short of humor, and a long awkward silence filled the steeple. The light bulb fizzled as if it only had a few more minutes left in it. "Look," he spoke up to fill the quiet, "I have no right to tell you what to do or how to feel. But maybe this will help you figure out that your bear thing is pretty small in comparison to some of the secrets people lug around."

They sat there for a long, raw moment. Then, her whole face changed. He was sure even the light bulb flickered with the flash of her eyes. "So, tell," she said with something he could only describe as quiet certainty. "I will if you will."

It was both the best and the worst dare he'd ever had.

Chapter Thirteen

December twentieth. Christmas Eve was four days away. Mary let the glorious tones of Handel's "Messiah" seep into her spirit as she sat on her couch and watched the flames on the trio of candles she had lit. The aroma of spiced cider filled out the sensory splendor of her Sunday evening.

It was the kind of night she'd have never sought in Chicago. For a woman who'd lived alone since grad school, Mary hadn't realized how much she'd avoided being alone. She was always filling time with things—arranging events, working late, playing in ensembles or participating in work-related social events. After all, it was much easier to avoid the emptiness with such a full schedule.

You did this, Mary said within her spirit. Communication with God on such a natural, conversational level had been such a surprise to her at first. Prayers were once elaborate verbiage to be recited, now prayer had become the sharing of thoughts and feelings with her Creator. *Alone is different for me now.* She'd read somewhere about the difference between "aloneness" and "solitude," thinking it only semantics then. She understood—or was coming to understand—the blessings of solitude. I'd still like a cat, she mused, wondering what God would think of something so close to a joke.

What would Curly think of that? It was an amusing question, but it brought her thoughts to a far more serious topic. What about Mac? A week of solitude wouldn't untangle her thoughts on the subject of that man and what he'd revealed to her yesterday. She'd had the feeling their lives had collided since the day they met, but she was powerless to say what sense it all made. Some days it made lots of sense and she could see things they held in common. Other days it seemed like they had no business even living on the same planet, much less taking up space in the same building. Why'd he tell me those things? She knew way too much about him now—things no one else knew. Yet.

Is that what You planned? That bargain that jumped out of my mouth after he told me? That didn't even feel like me. That was some other woman, some braver, stronger woman. Since that moment, Mary felt as if she'd set some terrifying sequence in motion. A part of her could grasp the good that would come out of it, but most of her just couldn't get past the process that would have to come first. *I don't know how I'm going to do this, Lord. No idea at all. Is this one of those things I just have to trust to You?* "Your move, Lord," she said out loud as she blew out the candles and got ready for bed. "I know I'm stumped."

Monday was supposed to be her day off, but with the drama only days away, today would have to be a workday. Even so, she'd planned to go in at noon and work clear through the "loading in" of the set into the sanctuary space tonight. Costumes, sets, lighting and the other myriad technical aspects of a small production had to come together in the next hour. *"Well, Lord,"* Mary thought as she pulled her thick hair into a practical braid down her back, *"thank goodness it's not a musical."* She stared at the mirror, amazed at the woman of her reflection casually conversing with God. The Lord Almighty who used to be carefully contained in Sunday services now seeped effortlessly—and wonderfully—into all her days and hours. Does it ever get old? Is it always this wondrous?

Her thoughts were interrupted by a knock on the door. Evidently the sets weren't going to wait until noon—surely something had gone wrong already, even though her phone hadn't rung yet. She stood on tiptoe to peer through the peephole, expecting Pastor Dave or Janet or Emily with a list of problems.

Instead, she saw Mac, smiling sheepishly with both hands in his pockets as she opened her door. "Do you have a minute to come to my office? I think we ought to talk."

Mary had been thinking the same thing. It seemed odd and uncomfortable to leave things where they had. "Sure," she said, tucking her keys into her pocket as they walked downstairs into the foyer that joined her stairway with the cut-through entrances to both Mac's office and Dinah's bakery.

Mac opened the door to his office, and she noticed a bakery box and two cups of coffee on the small conference table in his front window. Mac motioned to a seat and walked over to pull the string on the white bakery box. "I don't like to think on an empty stomach, so I got us something Dinah called 'Yuletide Blend' and a generous supply of gingerbread beings."

"Beings?"

"Dinah doesn't do just gingerbread men. Diversity, you know." He tilted the box toward her. "There's a whole gingerbread population in there—boys, girls, cats, dogs, horses, cows, you name it."

He wasn't kidding. It was as if the woman used every cookie cutter in the bluegrass region. She picked up a gingerbread pig sporting a red and green frosting bow and couldn't help but laugh. "Only Dinah."

"She's something, that's for sure. Nothing's ever ordinary with her." Mac's phone rang, and he glanced over to its display. "Rats, I have to answer this, but it'll only take a second. Have at that pig while you're waiting. Middleburg's the only place in America where you can munch on a Christmas gingerbread pig, so enjoy it while you can."

She scanned his office while he spoke briefly on the phone and hovered over his fax machine. A collection of certificates and awards took up one wall, along with a few requisite photos of Mac and probably officials holding shovels at groundbreaking ceremonies of one sort or another. A bookshelf hosted a collection of car books—coffee table photograph books about sports cars, a row of tiny toy cars and a pair of parts catalogs. She could picture him zipping down the road in that little convertible on summer days, even though it had hardly been warm enough for a ragtop since she'd moved here.

Thornton drove a fierce-looking black Italian sports car. It would stand out on Ballad Road twice as much as Mac's orange one, because while Mac's car looked fast and fun, Thornton's car looked like a predator.

There was another photo—several of them, actually—of Mac on a high mountaintop. The kind taken with a camera timer, showing him tanned and grinning in the middle of vast wildernesses. They'd not really talked about it, but she could easily guess that the reason Mac could be "on" so much—be so public, so talkative, so engaged—was because of the reservoir of private time and space he guarded so closely.

Thornton, on the other hand, had no wells to tend and didn't care about depth anyway. While the energy looked similar to Mac's on the outside, Thornton's vitality was a get-all-you-can-before-you-die hoarding, a frantic consumption of things and people. *Lord,* she wondered silently, *could I have seen that before You? Does faith give me new wisdom? Will You help me know what to do now?*

Mac scanned the paper, signed it and then fed it back into the machine. As the page hummed its way through the fax, Mac took a deep drink of his own cup. "Dinah says with enough sugar and caffeine you can save the world." He settled into the chair and pulled a black leather notepad in front of him. "I'm a bit weirded out after last night. I thought maybe we should talk some more. How are you? Okay?"

"Yes. And no. I mean, I'm calmer than I thought I'd be at the thought of telling people. But I'm still, well, 'weirded out' like you said."

"Look," he explained, "I meant what I said. I have no right to tell you what to do. But I do think you're underestimating Middleburg. No one's going to slam you for giving their kids a case of Bippo Bear fever."

He was awfully sure of her reception for a man in his position. "Well, I'm not as sure as you," she countered, "after all, your reaction wasn't exactly rosy."

"I'm an idiot. And that was before I knew it was you. I made fun of Drew Downing's TV show before he moved to Middleburg, too, so don't take it personally." He opened the notepad. "I wanted to show you something. A little crisis management tool I invented called the Mac Five. I think this is definitely time to fire it up."

"The Mac Five?" It sounded like a music group.

"Silly name, sound thinking. Watch." He grabbed a pen and began drawing a diagram of sorts, a circle with five circles around it. "This is the MacCarthy crisis management protocol, affectionately known as the Mac Five. Any situation has a first step to the solution, and most times it involves finding the five people who need to know first. Then, you can get them all together to figure out what to do next. Never thought I'd be using it on such a personal level…." He started to say something else, but bit his tongue.

Mary didn't know what to think. This didn't seem like the kind of situation that boiled itself down to a diagram. She didn't remember asking him for advice on how to reveal her past. Then again, she couldn't remember Mac asking before doing anything.

He raised one tawny eyebrow at her suspicious expression. "No really, hear me out. It applies. Lots of bad news gets delivered in my line of work. Things go wrong all the time. I realized last night—actually about two this morning—that this isn't much different." He wrote "Mary" in the center circle, then pushed the pen and pad across to her. "Humor me. Pick five people you think you might be able to tell. Just five."

The first person was obvious; Pastor Dave should be told. He knew a little bit about her former job, but certainly not about her particular bear-related achievements. Emily was one of the few people she'd classify as her friend in Middleburg, so she wrote her down. Drew and Janet fell easily into that group as well, especially since Drew's past as a public figure might give him particular insight into handling her problem. There, she'd filled in more than half the circles. Mac's crazy method seemed to have some value, for a thin layer of calm really was working its way into her as she wrote down names. Each circle she filled in helped her brain come up with a new idea. "Dinah and Cameron have been so nice to me, I think they'd react okay." Somehow she'd convinced herself that she didn't have friends in Middleburg yet, but that was wrong. And while it felt horrible and vulnerable to tell the whole world about her connection with Bippo Bears, she could handle these people knowing. Maybe I could, she realized, sitting up straighter and even reaching for another cookie. Maybe I could tell them and it'd be all right.

"There's something about getting it down on paper, isn't there?" He confirmed, taking the pad from her and tearing off the sheet. "I learned that from my dad my first week in business."

Mary looked at the diagram. "I don't know about the last circle. Sandy maybe?"

"Could be. I always try to think, 'Who's a stakeholder?' You know, who is or just considers themselves to have a stake in the problem."

She cringed at the thought; that reasoning led straight to Howard. He'd considered himself the catalyst that brought her here. And he was not the kind of man who cared to hear news secondhand. As judgmental as she feared he would be, she feared his reaction would be far worse if he wasn't told. With a heavy sigh, she filled in the last circle with Howard's name.

Mac let out a sigh, as well. "I had the same thought, I just didn't want to tell you what to do."

She gave him a doubtful look. "That one feels the worst."

"He might surprise you," Mac theorized, attempting a smile. "He's a man who appreciates results, and no one can argue you haven't seen spectacular results with that song."

"Spectacular?" That wasn't the word she'd have chosen.

"Well, maybe just 'big.' Plus, Howard's been known to play the indulgent grandfather a time or two. He may have even been a customer."

Mary shut her eyes against the vision of Howard glaring down a young mother over a store's last Bippo Bear. She found it disturbing to think of people she knew buying the toy. That was one of the things that had let her know it was time to leave. She used to love the idea of friends eating Jones Bars or Paulie's Pizza. She was proud of that work. She could never find it in herself to be proud of the Bippo Bear campaign. Mac, however, had not only succumbed to the campaign, he'd been a prime result—indulgent uncle shelling out far above the retail price to score a Bippo Bear. "What about you?" she asked, her pen hovering over the paper. "Since you already know, where do you go?"

He paused for a long, cumbersome moment, then slid Mary's page in front of him. Pulling another pen out of his shirt pocket, he drew a little line, sectioning off a bottom slice of the circle that held her name, so that it was sitting on the line. Under the line he wrote "Mac" in large, wide letters. "Right underneath you." He looked up at the ceiling. "Same as always."

He held her gaze for a moment, and she felt something deep down inside slide into place. Sure, his design was a useful crisis management tool, but that wasn't why she felt stronger. A quintet of circles didn't suddenly undergird her confidence. It was this man, this baffling, full-of-surprises man who dared to stick his neck out right alongside her. And, truth be told, had a far bigger secret with far darker consequences than the one she hid. "I still don't get why you're doing this," she remarked softly.

"Maybe it's just time I really *be* a leader instead of just acting like one." He kept his eyes on her. "But sometimes, God shows you something you don't want to see and somehow you know down deep what it is you need to do. It's the whole point of faith."

"It's terrifying," she confessed, wishing she could borrow some of the confidence in his eyes.

"It never stops being terrifying, you just get a little more used to it."

"You look so calm."

"I fake it well. I'm petrified on the inside."

Mary didn't think he looked it. Unnerved, maybe, just by the way he fidgeted with the pen or the way his easy smile wasn't quite as easy. But not the deer-in-headlights panic she was fighting. "Who's on your chart?" she asked before she realized what a personal question that was.

Mac leaned over and pulled out a folded piece of paper from his jeans pocket. "Funny that. It might look a bit familiar…." He unfolded the paper to reveal five circles around his name.

With the exact same names as hers.

Without a word, Mary took the paper from him and drew a line over the top bit of the circle with his name on it. She wrote "Mary" above the line, so that his center circle matched hers. "I got your back, Mac," she volunteered, managing a small laugh.

"Technically," he corrected and chuckled, "you've got my head."

She threw him a teasing look. "Don't get technical."

Chapter Fourteen

Mary made an "appointment" to talk with Pastor Dave for the following morning, and he met her with a cup of coffee as she returned the baby Jesus doll to the manger on the set. She'd stayed up late to sew the right arm back onto the doll. Last night Tommy Lee Lockwood, determined to buck his angel-role status when it didn't entail as much high flying as he'd hoped, had flung the poor Savior clear across the sanctuary in a fit of anger. It was one of those moments where the entire room fell silent, aghast that anyone—even an angry eight-year-old—would consider catapulting the baby Jesus into the choir loft. Mac tried to lighten the moment with a joke about next year's softball team. Howard pinned Tommy Lee's already-embarrassed mother with a disgusted stare. Emily gave out an exasperated sigh loud enough to be heard in Louisville.

While surprised, Mary tried to remember all the appalling things soprano divas had done during her musical career and calmly sent Tommy Lee up into the choir loft to fetch back the Christ child. Things deteriorated when "fetching back" simply meant flinging the doll back down from the choir loft, resulting in a physical separation that gave new meaning to "the right hand of God." Even though they still had two more scenes to get through, Mary had declared the rehearsal over. It didn't exactly do wonders for her confidence regarding this meeting.

"Tough crowd last night," Pastor Dave said as he eased himself down on the edge of the stage. "You're not here to tell me you're quitting, are you?"

It hadn't even occurred to her that he might interpret her request to meet that way. "Oh, no. We might not open on Broadway, but things'll pull together in the next two nights. Although, I'd be lying if I said I wasn't really looking forward to the potluck."

"Because it means your job will be over? Well, the harder part of your job?"

"A bit," she admitted. "But I also don't think I can skip town without tasting Howard's award-winning yuletide chili."

Pastor Dave leaned in. "His wife makes it, but we'll keep that little secret between ourselves, shall we?"

Secret between ourselves? God had handed her a blatant opening for the conversation she had in mind. "Funny you should mention secrets." She took a sip of coffee, shooting up a prayer for courage. This was so ridiculously hard. It didn't help that this morning's television news had broadcast a story of some poor Texas family putting their son's Bippo Bear up for sale on the Internet because the dad had been laid off this week. She was ready to turn off the television until New Year's—facing another Bippo Bear news story felt beyond her strength. "I...I have something to tell you," she began weakly.

"I gathered that," he said without a hint of judgment or worry in his voice.

Mary tried to take courage in his gentle demeanor. If the man hadn't excommunicated Tommy Lee for dismembering baby Jesus, maybe he'd take it better than she feared. "You need to know some things about my job before I came here." Mary took a deep, shaky breath. "And the man I used to work for."

"You already told me you worked for an advertising agency. I've never met anyone before you who made television commercials. Sounds rather exciting."

Thornton Maxwell wasn't exciting, he was frightening. "Well, yes, but it's more complicated than that."

"Why don't you tell me how?" She was hedging and he knew it.

"Well, Thornton Maxwell—my former boss—is a powerful man."

Pastor Dave gave an encouraging smile and glanced upward. "My boss is powerful, too. I think we can handle Mr. Maxwell. Has he done something to you?"

He looked so kind, so calm, Mary told herself to spit it out. Just say it. It's not as bad as you think, just blurt it out. Her mouth felt like it was full of cotton; words refused to form.

Dave put down his own mug. "Mary, would it help if I told you last night isn't the worst behavior I've seen out of this feisty little flock? I'm hard to shock anymore. But by the look on your face, you're about to admit to me that you're a government spy or a jewel thief."

He was trying humor, trying to make her comfortable. It made it all the worse. This looked so easy on Mac's diagram. She rolled her eyes, disgusted with her own ridiculous fear. "I wish."

Pastor Dave stared at her. "You *wish?*"

"Those sound less embarrassing. I think you'll find this crime a bit more…well…odd."

"Crime? What's going on, Mary? Just tell me."

"I did very particular work for Maxwell. It's musical. Sort of."

"So it's a…a musical crime?"

"Yes, and no. Well, you might find a few parents looking to lynch me—especially this week."

He shot her a look that let her know she wasn't making any sense. Of course she wasn't making any sense. All of this defied any sense whatsoever. Mary wiped her hands down her jeans and took a deep breath. "You see, I'm really, really good at writing advertising music." She had to say the *J* word. This should be like a bandage—just rip it off fast and get the worst pain over. "Jingles." She blurted it out. "I write ad jingles for kids. I…I wrote the Bippo Bear jingle. Those brawling parents? I did that. Those black-market Bippo Bears going for hundreds of dollars? I did that. It's me."

There was an enormous, awful silence. "You're telling me," Pastor Dave restated slowly, "that your crime against humanity is the Bippo Bear jingle?"

"Yep. Everything bad about Christmas wrapped up into one highly effective forty-second ditty. Mine. Miserable parents and disappointed kids everywhere? My doing. They'll be flinging *me* headfirst into the choir loft when people find out."

"You think people will blame you for what's going on over these bears?"

"I *am* responsible. I created the craze." Once the admission was out, Mary felt words tumble from her mouth in a nervous gush. "Just because it was my job doesn't mean it was right. My job was to fire up a frenzy with an annoying song kids could instantly memorize and endlessly sing to their parents. Get it? My job description was to give kids the tools to make their parents miserable and desperate. And I did it really well. So well I'll probably never live it down."

Pastor Dave took a long drink of coffee. "So, you're public enemy number one this week, hm? Hated by parents around the globe? A virtual catalyst for bad behavior and everything that's wrong about Christmas?"

Weren't pastors supposed to make people feel better? She hadn't expected him to welcome the news with open arms, but Mary expected something a little more understanding than this. "Um, yeah." A lump rose up in the back of her throat. She couldn't even look him in the eye.

He's going to fire me right here, Mary realized. Two days before Christmas and I'm going to get the boot.

"You can't have this job."

Oh, Lord, You can't let him fire me. "I know. I'm sorry about everything."

"The job of taking on the sins of the world is already filled. You can't have it."

She looked at him.

"I can't vouch for how well everyone in Middleburg will take the news—I did hear someone griping at Gina Deacon's diner just the other day—but I don't think your life is in danger. And I think you've let yourself whip up a whole lot of worry over something that doesn't warrant it."

Okay, maybe it wasn't the torment she had imagined. But he was a pastor, he was bound by certain codes of loving-kindness, wasn't he? "I don't think everyone will see it your way. I heard one of those women on the television. She was calling 'those advertising lowlifes' a couple of names I won't repeat in this sanctuary."

Pastor Dave sighed. "You won't be everyone's favorite. But no one is. You opened the door to a lot of bad behavior in your former job, but it's not that different. Part of my job is to hold up a mirror to folks' bad behavior. And while I admit I get an occasional dose of 'shoot the messenger,' it happens less than you think." He leaned back against a set wall. "Would you say that Bippo Bear campaign was a wake-up call for you?"

"Definitely. That campaign—and how delighted Thornton was with it—showed me things about my job I couldn't stand anymore. Not after I came to faith. Now, I can't understand how I found it so attractive. It feels so empty…even the money. Thornton used to say 'we breed greed' and we all smirked like that was a great thing. I'm ashamed." There. She'd said it.

"You're right. You're ashamed. Shame can be one of God's most effective weapons—when only He gets to wield it. It's we down here who tend to do harm with it. Me? I'm not so sure you're the criminal you make yourself out to be." He stood up. "I, for example, am simply giving thanks to God that He's refocused your fine talents in a better direction." He extended a hand to her, winking. "Of course, I ain't shelled out big bucks for a bug-eyed blue bear, neither. Matt Lockwood might have a thing or two to say to you."

"Tommy Lee wants a Bippo Bear?"

"Tommy Lee has a little sister. One who learns fast."

"Oh." Mary almost managed a chuckle. It was as if life had loosened its choke hold on her neck. Someone knew. Two people knew, actually, and neither one of them hated her. Maybe it wasn't really as dark a secret as she had thought.

They began walking to the church offices. "Am I the only one who knows?"

"No," she admitted. "Mac found me one day after Thornton sent me a warning of sorts."

Pastor Dave stopped walking. "A warning? What do you mean?"

In all her worry over the jingle, she'd not even mentioned her former boss's nastier tendencies. "Well, as you can imagine, Thornton wasn't thrilled to lose me. People generally don't walk away from his agency—until he fires them, that is. I didn't tell him where I am now because I didn't want him to come looking for me. But my last paycheck arrived at the apartment. So he knows."

"How do you reckon he found you?"

"This is an ad exec we're talking about. The man has ways."

Pastor Dave pinched the bridge of his nose. "Mary, you should have come to me earlier with this. I don't take to the idea of you dealing with this all by yourself."

"But I haven't been. Mac's been helping…." She realized that for the admission it was as soon as it left her mouth.

"Yes," Pastor Dave said with a knowing smile, "then there is Mac."

"No," she countered quickly, "it's not…"

"…anything I need to know at the moment," interjected Pastor Dave. "What I do need to know is what you think this Thornton fellow's intending. Is he just rattling your cage or does he have real harm on his mind?"

That really was the question, wasn't it? Was Thornton toying with her like the predator he was, dangling her a bit while he licked his chops, just to show he could crush her if he wanted to? Despite all his meanness, Thornton did have a very keen sense of just how cruel he could be and still fall within legal bounds. He'd only crossed that line once while she'd known him, and paid a whopping harassment fine as a result—crime doesn't pay especially when a senator's daughter is involved. "I'd feel a lot better if I could be sure," Mary admitted, "but I don't think he means harm. I think he just wants me to be miserable because I'm not working for him anymore."

Pastor Dave looked at her over the top of his circular gold glasses. "And are you miserable?"

"Only a bit." She smiled. "But only two people know so far. And there's two more days until Christmas."

He actually winked. "Miracles don't take long."

Mary should have settled down to work on some paperwork, but she couldn't. She had told Pastor Dave, and survived. Pastor Dave wasn't necessarily a barometer of how shorter-fused Middleburgians might take the news, but he hadn't fired her on the spot, either. As a matter of fact, he seemed to be fine with it. Thankful for the strength of her talents. She'd never thought to see it that way. *This is a good sign, Lord. One that ought to be shared.* She put her coat back on after fifteen minutes at her desk and told the church secretary she was going out to run last-minute errands.

That was true—she did have several things to pick up at the hardware store—but this trip was mostly about giving Mac a dose of good news. Humming to herself, she walked briskly down Ballad Road, turning to wave at Dinah as she pushed through Mac's office door...

...and right into a nasty argument in full-blown process between Mac and Howard. Mac's diagram hadn't worked out nearly as well for him.

"How many years are we talking about, MacCarthy?" Howard was bellowing. "Takes you over ten years to find your nerve?"

Mac was pacing the back of his office. "And I suppose you've never done anything but sheer upstanding conduct your whole life. C'mon, Howard, I was all of eighteen. I'm not having fun here, but I'm owning up to my stupidity. When's the last time you admitted you were wrong?" It was at this point that Mac even realized she'd entered the room. "Oh, no," he said, clearly unhappy to see her. He and Howard exchanged a series of warning looks. "Howard, don't," Mac said almost under his breath in a way that made Mary wonder how low the conversation had sunk before her arrival.

"And you, young lady," Howard spat as he turned to her. "Are you proud of your résumé? Tell me, do you find your job here sufficient penance for your part in the Christmas-profit machine? I hear Bippo Bears are going for upwards of $300 in Louisville."

All the glow of her conversation with Pastor Dave left the room in a wave of ice. "Mac?" she asked.

"I lost my cool," he explained, looking angry and miserable. "I'm sorry. Howard's infuriating."

As if that were an excuse. And how on earth had arguing with Howard over his teenage actions drawn him to spill her secret? The two topics weren't even mildly related.

"I stuck my neck out on your behalf," Howard said sharply. "I had a right to know."

"Bippo Bears have nothing to do with what Mary does at MCC," Mac shot back before she had a chance to say anything, which annoyed Mary further.

"Haven't you said enough already?" she snapped at him. "I'm not proud of what's happened with Bippo Bears, Howard. I agree it's the worst side of advertising. It's why I left. But I *did* leave."

"This reflects terribly." Howard scowled. "The whole church looks foolish. Have you seen the news lately?"

That was a ridiculous question. She felt like she'd been living the news with all the Bippo Bear frenzy coverage. Thornton probably had four full-time public relations people fielding press releases to every major news network, considering the coverage they were getting. "I'm miserable about it, Howard."

Howard glared at her. "At Gil and Emily's party, you didn't leave because you were tired, you left because all that Bippo business was on Gil's television. Grown people hitting each other over your toy. How can you sleep at night?"

"Cut it out, Howard, it's not her fault," Mac ordered, coming around the desk.

"You," Mary started, her own anger rising at Mac, "you had *no right*." She then turned to Howard, who was putting on his coat to go. Most likely to call an emergency meeting of the church council, if she knew him. Thank God she'd had the wisdom to go to Pastor Dave first. Maybe. Howard looked mighty sore at being caught unaware of what he considered a vital church issue. "Howard..." she began.

"Mary," said Mac.

"Mac!" She glared at Mac, letting her full fury show.

"I'm going to need to discuss this with Pastor Anderson," Howard announced. "And as for you, Mr. MacCarthy, I think perhaps we should take a good look at the legal fallout of what you've just told me."

"I've already talked to a lawyer, Howard. I'm not going to pretend this isn't serious. But I'd prefer to talk to Dave personally."

"I'll bet you would," Howard fired back. He glanced from Mac to Mary, obviously painting them with the same guilty brush. "The two of you."

"Don't go off half-cocked, Howard. It won't do anyone any good. Come back in here and let's try and have a reasonable conversation."

Mary could just imagine how "reasonable" the conversation would had gone. She wasn't feeling one bit reasonable and she'd been in the room for about thirty seconds. At the moment she wanted to beg Howard to keep quiet and to throttle Mac for not being able to keep quiet. She didn't need Thornton's help to have a miserable Christmas—misery was thriving just fine. Howard said some mumbling form of goodbye and nearly slammed Mac's office door shut behind him, leaving her to glare furiously at the man she'd come to encourage. Sufficient words just wouldn't come.

Mac was an unbearable combustion of frustration, anger and regret. He knew he'd lose his cool with Howard, he'd planned for what to do when Howard pushed his buttons—and he'd failed on all counts. He couldn't even remember how the conversation had bent itself in such a way that he revealed Mary's connection with Bippo Bears. He'd wanted to slam his head against the desk once the words slipped from his mouth, knowing full well the betrayal he'd committed. God had been especially cruel to see to it that she walked in at the moment she had—the ultimate in bad timing.

"How could you?"

He deserved every bit of the ice in her eyes.

"With all you knew, how could you tell him? Him!"

"I don't have an excuse, Mary. He got to me and suddenly I told him and I'm sorry." He'd never felt like such a lowlife.

"He'll tell everyone. He's probably on his way to Pastor Dave right now."

Which meant that Pastor Dave would hear what Mac had done to MCC from Howard. Worst possible scenario. Mac thought it served him right; whatever Dave thought of him based on Howard's revelation was nothing less than what he deserved. But Mary didn't deserve what he'd done to her, and his top priority now had to be to put things right with her if at all possible. Her current expression left little possibility. "Have you talked to him yet?"

"You know," she said, hugging her arms across her chest, "I was just coming in here to tell you how well it went. He was wonderful. Supportive." She leveled him with a hurt, furious look. "I was coming to tell you how right you were, coming to encourage you. Imagine that."

"Mistakes compound mistakes," Pa used to say, and Mac was feeling that in every bone in his body right now. His original mistake had been bad enough. Keeping it under wraps for a decade had made it worse. Now his attempt at confession had not only hurt him, but seriously hurt the person he was most trying to help. Not even a Mac-*Fifty*-five diagram could fix this. "I'm sorry," he apologized again, feeling the words woefully inadequate. "That was beyond stupid of me, and I'm so sorry." A crush of self-loathing pushed against his chest and made it painful to breathe.

"We have rehearsal tonight," she said in an unsteady, trying-not-to-cry voice that let him know he could actually feel worse than he already did. "I don't know how I'm… we're going to do this. I'm going to go upstairs and figure out what to do next."

"I…"

"Don't!" she snapped back at him, fisting her hands. "Don't talk to me."

He felt the slam of his office door as if it had busted

every one of his ribs. Worst of all, as he gathered up his coat and keys, he could just make out the sound of her crying as it came through the floorboards between them. Mac had seen buildings fall, timber splinter, dynamite explode through solid rock, but the sound of Mary Thorpe crying did the most damage of all.

Chapter Fifteen

Mac barreled down the pike in his car, taking turns too fast and downshifting the car so hard it shuddered. He slammed the coupe through its gears, not caring what road he took or where it led him. The stereo was up so loud it thumped in his chest. Taking his anger out on the road ahead of him, he drove recklessly, half hoping someone would pull him over and arrest him like the jerk he was. It wasn't until he missed a turn and sent the car skidding into a gravel-spitting spin that he pulled his temper back into check. He sat there, turned the wrong way of a deserted intersection, panting from the effort of holding the car through its spin, and let his head fall sharply against the steering wheel. It had all gone horribly wrong. Somewhere in the beginning of this mess he'd had good intentions. He'd run for mayor not only to push Middleburg toward its future, but to make up for his past. To prove to himself—and, he now realized, to Howard—that he wasn't that angry teenager anymore.

But he was.

Everything had been lost in the never-ending sin of his

short temper. Even the morning after the steeple fell, he'd never felt so utterly worthless. He banged the stereo knob with the heel of his hand, silencing the music to hear the echo of his own misery. He'd been so full of pride. So convinced of his ability to make the world a better place. And now look at you. At what you've done. *Lord, I wouldn't be half surprised if You washed Your hands of me right this minute.*

His cell phone rang. He ignored it.

It rang again. On the third time, he fished it out of his coat pocket to see Gil Sorrent's name on the screen. Here we go.

Gil didn't bother with a greeting. "Where are you?" He knew. Mac could hear it in his voice.

Mac didn't even know. He looked up, squinting at the route signs. "About a dozen miles out of town, I suppose."

"Did you do it?" There was no need for any clarification of details. Mac knew exactly what Gil was asking and why.

"Yes." Mac wiped one hand down his face and groaned. "I've messed this up something fierce. I don't know what to do."

"Come to the farm."

Gil was right. The office was no place to go now. "Sure, in twenty minutes, tops. But I think I'd better drive a little slower than I have been." In some sick desire to feel as bad as possible, he asked, "Who knows?"

"By the time you get here, probably everyone. Howard ain't much for being subtle when he's mad."

Mary's imagined lynch mob had come to life. Her overblown fear about people's conceptions of her Bippo Bear involvement would get mixed in with their justified anger over his secret, and the whole thing would get tumbled together in a Christmas nightmare. "Mary…"

"Emily's on the phone with Dinah now, sending her up to Mary's apartment to stay with her until we all figure out what to do next."

What to do next? That didn't really need a lot of planning. Mac had to stand and face the music, that's what happened next. There was an odd, almost hysterical freedom to having the whole process ripped from his hands. Mac was smart enough to realize he had very little control over how things played out from here. It could be everything from a touching reconciliation to a lawsuit to being run out of town—Mac resigned himself to whatever God handed him as a consequence for his actions.

Mary, however, was another story. She'd brought none of this on herself. She was working through a highly emotional issue in the best way she knew how. God was clearly at work within her, and he'd made it all worse instead of offering the help he'd intended. Faith was still a new underpinning for her life—it had caught some tender part of him to watch her reliance on God grow. He'd barely realized how much he'd come to care for her.

That is, of course, until he hurt her in the worst possible way. He'd always been able to smooth over his outbursts with a clever remark, a funny story, or even a prank to bring people back onto common ground. A hundred clever comebacks would never save him from this betrayal. He'd known that God had trusted him with the precious secret of Mary's situation. Known the delicate nature of her new faith and her new place in this community. And he'd done it terrible harm.

The fact that Howard goaded him into it wasn't even close to an excuse.

Mac wasn't surprised to see Pastor Dave's car in the drive in front of Gil's house. Nor was he surprised to see the look of supreme disappointment on Gil's face when he opened the door. Gil said nothing, just nodded and ushered Mac into the huge den. Before its massive fireplace, Mac remembered, was where Homestretch Farm conducted all of its most serious business. Well, thought Mac, this qualifies.

Pastor Dave looked tired. "This isn't fair to you," Mac offered as he took one of the large leather chairs that circled the hearth. "I'm sorry."

Pastor Dave took off his glasses and ran a hand across his eyes. "I'd much rather have heard this from you." Mac could only imagine Howard's rendition. He started to give his version of the story, then thought better of it. Whatever evils Howard had ascribed to him, he probably deserved them.

"I had planned to tell you…next." It sounded so weak, even if it was true. "I thought Howard needed to hear it first. It was his car that was damaged, after all. It was a terrible decision to keep this to myself all these years."

Emily entered the room, carrying mugs of coffee for the group. "Why now? What made you bring this up two days before Christmas?"

"It was Mary, actually."

Gil looked up as he took a mug from Emily. "Mary?"

"She was so terrified about what you all would think of her when you knew about the Bippo Bears. The secret was making her crazy. At first I just wanted to help, to let her know everyone has things they hope no one finds out. Then I realized I wasn't much better. It was like God used her as a mirror to hold up against my own secret—if that makes any sense. I thought if she could see me survive mine, she'd know she'd survive hers."

"What's Mary got to do with Bippo Bears?"

Mac was not going to open his mouth. He was not going to heap more onto his whopping pile of betrayal, useless as it was now. He looked at Pastor Dave, silently asking him how much should be said.

"Mary's job before she came to Middleburg was with an advertising agency. Mary is the person who wrote the Bippo Bear jingle. She feels personally responsible for all this nonsense going on over these bears. And she's pretty sure you all won't think too highly of her when you find out."

Gil and Emily exchanged surprised glances. News of Mary's supposed "sins" hadn't reached them yet evidently. "That silly Bippo Bear song? The one in the commercials? That's Mary's?" Emily asked, taking a mug for herself and sinking into a chair.

"It's a dumb song and I'm sick of it, but how is it her fault?" Gil inquired.

"Her job," Mac explained, "was to write a song kids could sing to their parents that would get stuck in their heads. To create that kind of 'I want it' fever so parents would do whatever it took to get their kids a Bippo Bear for Christmas."

"It worked," Gil replied. "I hate that song and I don't even have kids." He paused a moment before adding, "yet."

Emily looked between Mac and Pastor Dave. "He knows. Actually, except for Dinah, we're the only four who do. Oh, and Mary—I told her when she cast me as Mary."

"Her boss basically charged her with writing a song that would incite parents to riot," Pastor Dave described before taking a sip of his coffee. "She did her job. Actually, it's part of why she left advertising altogether. Once she came to faith, that sort of thing stuck in her craw. I admire her— she took a big risk to act on her convictions."

One I failed to take for years. Mac chided himself silently. "She's miserable. She saw the way we've been trashing the Bippo Bear people—come on, everyone's been harping on them, even me. I mean, I paid big bucks for one of those things for my nephew and I told folks I was steamed they were in such short supply. You couldn't find one anywhere, and that made them easy scalping. And then when the fights were shown on television, what was she supposed to think? That we'd all compliment her on a job well done?"

"She's supposed to think that we're smart grown-ups who know the difference between an advertising campaign and a toddler tantrum." Emily replied sharply. "I'm embarrassed. Do we come off that judgmental? Does she really think we'd hang her over Bippo Bears?"

"Maybe not hang her," Pastor Dave clarified, "just fire her off the church staff. And, I'm afraid, she's not too far off the mark. Howard ain't exactly a bundle of mercy at the moment."

"Why on earth did you tell Howard about Mary and the Bippo Bears?" Emily asked, making Mac feel even lower than he already did.

"I wasn't supposed to. Howard just…was Howard." Mac relayed the whole argument, how Howard called him a coward, a "poor reflection of the community's fine character" that should "never be allowed to run for office," which goaded Mac into a few choice remarks about Middleburg's character, which led to how they'd made Mary afraid for her secret, and so on. "He pushed my buttons and I got stupid," he said as he concluded his account of their argument and how Mary walked in at the worst possible moment. "I ought to know better than to let Howard get to me like that. I hurt her and I have no excuse for what I did."

"Howard," Pastor Dave said while he sighed, "feels the church had a right to know before we hired her. He feels betrayed, and worries all this bear ridiculousness will reflect badly on the church."

"I'll tell you what will reflect badly on MCC," Emily replied. "If we treat her like some kind of criminal just because she used to do what she used to do—that'll reflect badly on the church. I can't believe people think like that!"

"I can," Gil admitted sadly. "I overheard folks in Deacon's Grill the other day. People are steamed about all the press these bears are getting. They keep running ads even though no one's got any more to sell. Can't say I haven't thought the same thing, but I wouldn't take it out on Mary personally."

"She doesn't know that," Mac revealed. "She has no way of knowing that."

"I think," offered Pastor Dave gently, "that we're getting off the topic of what to do about you, Mac. You've got a serious issue on your hands. If anything, you may be a blessing to Mary, taking the focus off her." Mac hadn't thought about it that way, but it didn't help much.

"Stuffed animals aren't exactly the same level of seriousness as deliberate vandalism to a church," Pastor Dave continued. "And a car."

"*Howard's* car," Gil reminded the room, although Mac surely didn't need reminding. "He could press charges, I suppose, but I would think the statute of limitations has run out by now."

"Are you ready, Mac, to stand up and deal with this?" Pastor Dave asked Mac with seriousness in his eyes. "To everyone? Tonight?"

"I have to. I don't really see how this can wait until after Christmas." This'll go down as my worst Christmas ever,

Mac thought to himself. "We need to deal with this now. Tonight's a good as any, although I think it'll blow any chance of rehearsal clear out the window."

"Well, then," Pastor Dave continued, standing up, "I think it's time for God to show up in big and mighty ways." He set down his mug with a nod of thanks to Emily and reached for his coat. "I think it's high time I go check on Mary."

"Tell her I'm sorry," Mac relayed, catching the pastor's elbow.

"I think you ought to do that yourself. You two have a fair amount to work out before either one of you come to rehearsal, I'd say." Dave checked his watch. "It's two now, so why don't I tell Mary you'll come by at around four?"

Mac nodded, just as his cell phone went off. "I have a feeling that's Ma," he guessed, reaching into his pocket. It was. These days, the only thing that could outpace his car was the speed of small-town gossip. "I'd better get over there." He extended a grim hand to Gil. "Start praying. I think God's about to take me down a peg—or six." He leaned down and gave petite Emily a peck on the cheek. "Congratulations," he spoke softly. "I haven't had a chance to say that yet. I'll try to straighten out my act by the time the little fella gets here. If you'll still have me." It stuck in his throat with an unexpected lump.

"Nonsense," Gil objected, leveling a serious look right in Mac's eyes. "God's just gettin' started on you—I expect big things on the other end of this mess."

"See you tonight," Emily vowed, squeezing Mac's hand. "We'll be there. Promise."

"Mary, talk to me. We've got to talk about this." Mac had been outside her door for ten minutes now. A more mature woman, someone with years of solid faith under her belt, might have been able to open up that door to the man who'd betrayed her worst secret, but Mary was not there yet. She looked at her dining room table, where the envelope from her parents' house lay open. Thornton had sent hard copies of four different e-mails. Four different media outlets asking for interviews with "the creator of the Bippo Bear jingle." He'd mailed them, along with a Christmas bonus and a personal note asking for her return to Maxwell Advertising, to her in care of her parents even though she knew he now had her Middleburg address. It was a masterful manipulation— wrapped in loyal employer language that would coddle her parents, but letting *her* know he could go public at any moment. Mary knew the only reason he *hadn't* was that the mystery somehow served his purpose. The duplicity of it all made it worse than the outright blackmail she'd suspected from him.

Which made Mac just like Thornton. She'd allowed herself to believe she could expect loyalty from Mac, and instead he'd done the one thing he knew would hurt her most. No, she couldn't open the door and face that man. He'd hurt her worse than anything Howard could have said, because she'd allowed herself to care about Mac. She looked at the paper with the circle diagram as it sat next to Thornton's clever note, remembering the tenderness of Mac's voice as he said, "Right underneath you, same as always," and she wanted to crumple the thing and send it into the fireplace to burn. "Go away," she said to the door with as much strength as she could muster, then she walked into her living room and turned up the stereo loud enough to drown out any persuasion he might try next.

Chapter Sixteen

$\mathbf{M}$ac felt like the very air in the church sanctuary was on the verge of combustion. The whole building had a surreal dissonance to it—the joyful decorations at odds with his miserable spirit. The sanctuary looked amazing. Each of the stained glass windows were framed in fragrant pine boughs frosted with dozens of tiny white lights, and each window sill hosted a trio of hurricane candles circled in holly and red ribbon. The set, while nothing that would turn heads on Broadway, was brilliantly colored and made the church look, well, happy. *Everything* looked happy. The trouble was nothing *felt* happy.

After all that preparation, Mac felt as if he was standing on the brink of the worst Christmas ever. It was ten minutes past the hour, and no one had seen Mary all afternoon. *Take care of her, Lord—I sure can't. You know how much I wanted to go into this with things settled between me and her.* Still, it wasn't as if he had the right to have things the way he wanted. This mess—large or small—was his own doing.

Mac stood up. There was no chance he could feel

worse, and it was time to take this mistake into his own hands anyway. Howard stood up seconds after Mac rose off his chair, and for a moment there was a silent challenge as to who would take command of the room. Mac cleared his throat loud enough to make everyone in the room turn to look at him. Everyone, that is, who wasn't staring at him already. "I think," he announced as steadily as he could, "that we might as well tackle this here and now. It looks like rehearsal isn't going to happen, and I doubt anyone here is in the dark as to why."

Howard made some sort of gruff sound, but said nothing as Mac walked to the front of the room.

"Just in case you've been hiding under a rock for the last few hours, I did, in fact, admit to Howard that I was behind the steeple falling down during its construction twelve years ago. I was an angry kid who did something stupid. I reckon it will go down as one of my life's biggest mistakes—both then and now—but somehow I'd fooled myself into thinking it didn't really matter."

Howard coughed loudly, transmitting his disagreement.

"Well," Mac went on while looking Howard straight in the eye, "it matters a whole lot. I get that now. And it's up to me to put things right as much as I can. And I figure there are some parts of this that I can't put right, and I'll have to take that as it comes." He took a deep breath and thrust his hands into his pockets to stop the urge to fidget that suddenly overtook him. He shifted his eyes to several people around the room, catching some supportive expressions and others that were condemning. The duality of it matched his current emotions; this was at once both easy and horrible. Easy in that he hadn't even realized how the weight of this secret had pressed on him over the years and had now been released, and yet horrible in that it made him feel disliked and vulnerable and at the town's collective mercy. "First off, I'm sorry. I'm sorry I did it, I'm sorry I lied about it then and that I didn't come clean before now. I damaged Howard's car, the church and put people in danger. I didn't handle my anger well and I allowed it to let me do something wrong. And dangerous."

"Every one of us has done things we regret," Sandy Burnside acknowledged, looking around the room.

"Every one of us," repeated Matt Lockwood—father of the less-than-angelic Tommy Lee, "didn't hide it and then run for mayor. What else we gonna find out about you?"

"Hopefully, that I set things right when I can. Howard, I looked up the value of your car that was hit by the falling steeple, and I'm prepared to write you a check to cover those damages. Even the ones covered by your auto insurance." He'd planned to tell Howard this when he confessed to the deed earlier this afternoon, but the argument had spiraled out of control before he'd had the chance. "And I want to say I'm sorry, to you personally, here in front of everyone."

He paused briefly, hoping Howard might say something along the lines of "apology accepted," but Howard remained silently standing. Howard would probably accept the apology in the long run, but he wasn't the kind of man to do something like that quickly.

"Now I'd apologize to our former Pastor Donalds if I could, but I don't know where he moved to. I'm going to try to find him." Mac scanned the back of the room until he found Pastor Anderson. "But in the meantime, I'll apologize to Pastor Anderson for damaging the church the way I did, and I'm trying to work up some figures so I can pay MCC back in some way. You don't need a new steeple anymore, but I'm sure he'll find some use for the money."

"I accept your offer of restitution," Pastor Anderson responded with a formal tone. "On behalf of the congregation back then and the congregation now."

A few folks in the room looked like they weren't so ready to let it go at that, but no one actually said anything. The tension in the room changed to awkward mumbling that wasn't a riot, but wasn't quite silence, either.

"And then there's the other thing," Mac continued. Howard began moving toward the front of the room. "I think we need to get that out on the table now, too."

"There's more?" The alarm in town librarian Audrey Lupine's voice wasn't helping matters.

"It seems Mac was privy to some important information about Miss Thorpe," Howard interjected. "Information we should have known before we hired her."

"Information," Pastor Anderson added, "Mary was under no legal obligation to provide us. She gave us her employment history in all the detail we asked for."

"Matters of church staff go beyond legal obligations," Howard declared. "She had a moral obligation to tell us."

"Tell us what?" a woman who worked on the costumes asked.

"Haven't you heard?" said another woman in a less than kind voice. "About the Bippo Bears."

"Yes, Mary Thorpe is part of the Bippo Bear atrocity." Howard's tone was grave. "She worked to make those crazy blue bears into something every child wants. Into something that's starting fights at stores and turning Christmas into nothing more than a profit machine for some soulless toy manufacturer. That's the person we hired to run our Christmas drama. Someone who not only had that in her background, but purposely hid that from us because she knew the response we'd have to it."

Atrocity? Howard made it sound like she was out knocking small children down with a baseball bat. "See? This is exactly why she chose not to mention it. The woman was just doing her job for the advertising agency where she used to work. The one she left when her faith called her to do something else. The same faith that called her here," Mac informed.

"You're defending her?" said the first woman. "You?" As if he were the last person in the world who should stand up for Mary.

"He knew about it. He'd discovered her deception and didn't come forward. This is why I'm so angry. All of this shows an alarming lack of integrity. We've got to have people who look out for the public good running for office in Middleburg. I've said it before and I'll say it again, I'm not against someone running for mayor. I'm against the *wrong* person running for mayor. I'd say you've shown yourself to be the wrong person, MacCarthy."

Mac felt his blood begin to rise. "Back off, Howard. We're talking about Mary."

"You're both equally guilty."

"Y'all hang on a minute, the two of you." Sandy Burnside stretched out her hands between them like a referee. "Calm down. The way I see it, Mary wrote an advertising jingle. One she was paid to write. I can't see the crime in that."

"Have you heard that thing? I reckon it really could fix folks to riot," Vern from the hardware store chimed into the discussion. "Gets stuck in your head like a bad cold. My daughter spent her whole Christmas budget getting one of those things for my grandson just 'cuz he whined so much to get one. Crazy if you ask me."

Emily stood up. "But that's not Mary's fault. She's embarrassed about what's happened with the bears, and that's why she didn't tell us. She was afraid of what we'd think. And we've proved her right, haven't we?"

Gina Deacon spoke up. "I'm sick of hearing about it in the diner. Obviously, y'all find enough to fight about without adding some Christmas bear nonsense to the mix. I know for a fact she heard folks going on about how bad the ads were right in front of her face. I don't know that I blame her for keeping it quiet."

"We should have known. In advance," Howard countered. "She should have known it would become an issue, especially over the holidays. She showed poor judgment. Poor character. A person of integrity would have come forward immediately, knowing the nature of the situation." About one-third of the room nodded along with Howard. "It reflects poorly on the church and what it stands for this time of year."

"And what *does* the church stand for, Howard?" demanded Dinah Rollings, standing up and squaring off at Howard. "Where's the 'peace on earth, goodwill to men' in all of this?" She swept her hand around the room. "I doubt Jesus would be too pleased with what's gone on today. Lost tempers. Fights. People not being able to forgive each other or not owning up to things they've done. Folks afraid of other folks for no good reason. Calling each other's character into question and telling things that ought not to be told. This sure ain't the kind of Christmas I hoped for when I moved to Middleburg." Another third of the room nodded in agreement to Dinah. "How we're gonna pull off tomorrow night now, Lord only knows. I sure don't." With a dramatic huff, Dinah moved to the back of the room where she paced with annoyance.

Things were about to spiral out of control. "Look," said

Mac determined to pull out whatever stops it took to keep this from dissolving into disaster, "let's put everything on the table here. This play was a small bandage on a big wound and we all know it. I'm sorry I've upset you all, but if you want me to be sorry I ran—am running—for mayor, I won't. Maybe I'm not perfect. Maybe I messed this up on a global scale and some of you can't get past that. I can live with that. But what I can't live with is what we've done to Mary. We hired her for all the wrong reasons, Howard. We thought we could all distract ourselves from the real stuff by putting on this ideal Christmas drama—as if Middleburg would heal itself like one of those old movie musicals where the kids put on a show in Grandpa's barn and save the world. We put her in such an impossible situation that she was afraid to be part of our community. Afraid to let us know this tiny little detail—this ridiculous bear thing—that has her so frightened. She's ashamed of something she has no reason to be ashamed of. You know why I found the spine to tell Howard after all these years? Because I wanted to show her that Middleburg wouldn't hang her for a mistake. I figured if I 'fessed up to my actual criminal act and survived, that she'd realize she could let people know about the jingle and be fine. I was trying to help her let her secret loose, but I let Howard get under my skin and I told her secret instead. And that's low. Me, I deserve what I get. But Mary's done nothing but try and pull this thing together under impossible circumstances and she's deserved none of it. She's an amazing, talented woman who deserves to be welcomed into Middleburg as part of our community. Which, if you ask me, is what she needed most and why God sent her here." Suddenly realizing he'd made a very long speech, Mac shut up and sat down on the edge of the stage.

"Where is she anyway?" asked Sandy Burnside. "She's supposed to be here. Has anyone checked on her?"

"I just did," Dinah answered, pulling open the sanctuary's back doors. He hadn't even noticed her leaving the room—he was so busy speechifying. Dinah stepped aside to reveal Mary standing behind her. "She was coming in as I went out. Just in time to hear someone's big speech. And for once, I don't mean Howard's."

Every single eye in the room was on Mary. Her entrance into the room was as painful as she had expected—she couldn't for the life of her tell if the crowd was ready to welcome her or what. Some man in one corner looked down and shook his head. Pastor Anderson stood up slowly, as did Emily. Howard looked like he'd have crossed his arms over his chest again if they weren't already there. The sanctuary was excruciatingly silent.

"Well," acknowledged Sandy Burnside, "you're here. 'Bout time, too. So I suppose there's only one question worth asking now. Are you really the gal behind that troublesome little song?"

Mary caught Mac's eyes staring right at her. His eyes were a storm of fear, worry, regret, embarrassment—it surprised her that she could read his expression so clearly under such dire circumstances. Quite simply, he looked awful. Mary took a deep breath and stood up straighter. Some odd little part of her recognized she was about to finish off all the remaining circles in her Mac Five in one fell swoop. "Yes, I wrote the Bippo Bear jingle. I'm not proud of it, but there it is."

Tommy Lee Lockwood looked at her with an awed expression. "Cool."

She couldn't help but smile. "Not really."

One older woman Mary recognized from the choir shook a finger at her. "Aren't you ashamed of yourself?"

Mary thought it would be horrible the first time she faced someone like that. It wasn't as bad as she'd feared. "As a matter of fact, I am," she replied, amazed at the steadiness of her voice. After all, there really wasn't anything left to lose at this point. "I'm ashamed of whom I used to be. At what I used to think was important. But that's the point of faith, I think."

"I could go into a big speech of that being the whole point behind the coming of the Christ child," said Pastor Anderson, walking to the center of the room, "but I think we've heard enough speeches already." He turned to Mac. "Do you admit that you've made a mistake and you're willing to make up for it?"

Mac nodded. "Already have admitted it, and I've already offered to do whatever I need to do to set things right."

"Mary," continued Pastor Anderson, "do you admit it might have been wise to let us know what was going on in your professional life beforehand and that your fears and our alarm might have been avoided if we'd just talked about this earlier?"

"I suppose I've come to realize that's true, yes."

Pastor Anderson turned to Howard. "Do you admit to having an understandable reaction to some news but that you would be able to get past it, given a little time?"

Howard unfolded his arms and shifted his weight a bit before admitting, "That's a possibility."

Pastor Anderson swept his hands around the room. "Do all of you agree that maybe we've gotten our spirits out of joint here for any number of reasons? And that the only true solution to all of this is the Christ we're supposed to be welcoming?"

Janet stood up and crossed her hands over her chest. "It's Christmas," she declared in the take-charge voice of a stage manager. In fact, Janet had made an outstanding stage manager, and it didn't look like she was going to stop now. "If we can't find a way to get along at Christmas, then we should be ashamed of ourselves. Mary, I want us to rehearse. I've put too much into this to have it all go to pieces now. As far as I'm concerned, scene one starts in five minutes. Anybody else want to give it a try?"

As awful as everything was, Mary felt a surge of blessing to have Dinah and Janet in her corner. Emily, too. She'd been wrong thinking everyone would reject her.

She caught Mac's gaze over the crowd, and felt her own emotions tangle up with the tumult in his eyes. Everyone had made so many mistakes. Mac had hurt her, but he'd made that mistake in the process of trying to help her. There was a powerful pull in that. If she could feel that pull, even now after what he'd done, then wasn't there something important under all that human imperfection? Mary gave him the slightest of smiles, an "I'll try" slip of a smile, and she watched that tiny piece of encouragement light a spark in the green of his eyes.

Dress rehearsal went as well as could be expected under the circumstances: namely, a complete disaster. Cues were missed, baby Jesus, although now in possession of all his limbs, never made it onstage for the final scene so that Emily cradled a limp roll of cloth instead of the Almighty Savior. No one knew the Magi's bottle of frankincense was real glass until the actor dropped it and it shattered, sending Audrey Lupine running for the church first aid kit to bandage Shepherd Number Three's left hand. Howard and Mac were barely above useless, repeatedly forgetting lines in between mutual onstage "stare-downs" and a smattering of curt remarks. Mary found herself praying with all her might that the old adage "bad dress rehearsal, good opening night" was true.

She closed up the costume closet with an exhausted sigh, happy to find Pastor Dave just behind her with a mug of hot chocolate—the man seemed to specialize in "comfort muggings" as he jokingly called them. "Think we'll survive?" he asked, his tone a mix of humor and genuine concern.

"I've never felt less in control of anything in my entire life," Mary stated and leaned back against the wall, clutching the mug with both hands. "I've told God eleven times in the past thirty minutes alone that this is way beyond me. That only He can pull this off tomorrow night." She looked at the older pastor, amazed that he could be so calm when the world seemed to be spinning out of control. "I should be panicked out of my skin, but you know, I'm not. Maybe I'm just too tired to know I ought to be panicking."

Pastor Anderson chuckled and leaned back against the wall opposite her in the hallway. "Maybe God's getting through to you that it was His job to pull it off all along. We're stubborn folk this side of heaven. Sometimes I find God has to rip the control out of our hands to make us recognize we never had control in the first place. That place where you are? The place where it feels like, unless God shows up, you're sunk? Well, I find that's the place where God usually shows up. In big ways. Doing things no one expected."

"Oh," Mary said and sighed, "that would definitely be now."

"How do you feel now," Pastor Dave continued as they

started walking back up the stairs toward the sanctuary, "now that everyone knows?"

"Okay. Not okay. It's nice to know not everyone blames me. But I've gotten my share of dirty looks today—some people really do blame me. Except for Tommy Lee Lockwood. He's asked me four times if I can get him a bear."

"For his sister?"

"No, actually," Mary replied with an amused whisper. "He told me he could get twice what they're worth through some Internet site."

"Tommy Lee Lockwood's too young to think Kentucky has a black market," Pastor Dave observed and then laughed.

"Tommy Lee's too young for lots of the things he thinks and does if you ask me."

Pastor Dave stopped at the top of the stairs. "Vern Murphy tells me folks used to say that about young Joseph MacCarthy. Mac had a talent for trouble, but I think he turned out okay. He'll turn out okay when all this is over, too. It's the man who *doesn't* learn from his mistakes that you need to watch out for."

Mary didn't have a reply. She just nodded and sipped her cocoa again as they pushed open the sanctuary doors where her coat and script still lay along with a box of props that needed mending.

The sanctuary was dark except for a handful of small lights and the moonlight coming in through the stained glass windows, but it wasn't empty. A single figure sat at the front of the pews, head resting on one hand, shoulders hunched. Mac.

"Like I said," Pastor Dave whispered, turning back toward the hallway that led to the parking lot, "God shows up."

Chapter Seventeen

Mary felt a dozen different emotions as she walked up the aisle toward Mac. He turned and looked at her calmly, as if he'd been waiting. The expression in his eyes unwound something deep in her chest. Did she really have the capacity to forgive him? Or was she just too exhausted to be angry anymore? She sat down in the same pew, and for a moment they both looked at the rebuilt silver star that now hung in the top of the sanctuary. She remembered the time in the steeple, when they went to look for that star.

"I've been thinking," Mac said in a hoarse voice, "how to apologize to you, but everything I come up with falls short. What I did was awful. I should be able to say something meaningful, you know, eloquent, to make up for it. But all I keep thinking is that my run-on mouth is what got me into this to begin with." He looked up at her, his green eyes piercing the darkness. "I never meant to hurt you. Not in a million years. But I did, and I'm beyond sorry."

"Did you mean what you said earlier? That you first thought about telling your story to help me?"

"Yeah," he conceded. "Twisted as it was." He managed a weak laugh. "It didn't quite turn out the way I planned."

"Thanks. For trying to help, I mean." She surveyed the sanctuary, imagining the crowd of people who'd been in here earlier. "Everybody knows now and I'm still alive. I suppose in some respects you were right—it's not as bad as I thought it would be. I'd turned it into some kind of horrible thing in my mind."

"We can do that, you know. Twist things up in our minds. God can give us a good idea and we can foul it up something fierce." He paused for a moment before he leaned back in the pew and looked up at the ceiling. "Like running for mayor," he said softly. "I know God wanted me to run, but I thought it was so that I could be a big shot, the guy who could take on Howard."

"And now?"

"Now I know God wanted me to run so I could clean up my own house."

Mary wasn't quite sure what he meant by that. She leaned over to try and decipher the feelings exposed on his face, but the shadows hid his features. "How so?"

He turned toward her, and Mary felt her heart jolt at the sight of his expression. The man before her had been stripped of his bravado, of his clever words and fancy plans. This is what it felt like to look into someone's soul—unedited, unprotected, exposed. "I'm *not* ready to run for mayor. Maybe someday, but I've got a load of work to do on the inside before I try and change the world. I'll be thirty in seven days and I've never felt less grown up. I let one guy goad me into hurting someone I…someone I've come to care a whole lot about. That's not a guy who should be mayor."

Mary thought it would be a long, hard process, but it

wasn't. It was a single, clear moment that swept across her like a breeze. "I forgive you," she said, amazed how the words felt both large and effortless at the same time.

He looked at her with a startled amazement. "I wouldn't blame you if you didn't. I'm such a jerk—I think God allowed me to believe I was helping you because I'd have never 'fessed up on my own."

"Maybe God fixed it so you told because I'd have chickened out of telling on my own. I don't suppose that really matters at this point." She sighed. "Now what? The town's in worse shape than when I started."

"Oh, I don't know. Maybe this wasn't one of those things you could fix creatively. We had to tackle it up front, out in the open, ugly and all." Mac let his head fall back against the pew. "I think down deep we all still like each other. We've just got to find our way back to that."

That was it, wasn't it? Could she find her way back to the affection she felt for Mac after what he'd done? He'd said it himself, that his original intent had been to help. His failings had gotten in the way of his intent. Could she say much differently? Hadn't her original intent to do a good job been hampered by her own faults?

"I want to find a way back," she proclaimed, turning to him. A way back for Middleburg, and maybe even a way back for the two of them.

"Hanged if I know how," he admitted, more to the empty room than to her.

"Actually," Mary revealed, sitting up, "I think maybe I do."

"Oh," groaned Mac, "you're not talking about the potluck, are you?"

"Oh, I am. Besides," she concluded, amazed she could find it within herself to smile, "now you *have* to come."

* * *

This is my Christmas gift to myself. Mary took a deep breath, grabbed her phone and dialed the number the following morning.

"Mary, darling!" Thornton's overly dramatic greeting was too loud and too cavalier. He was almost shouting; she could hear the noises of a city bar in full swing behind him. "I just knew I'd be hearing from you today. How are you out in the middle of nowhere, wherever you are?"

It would be hard to pack more untruths into three short sentences: Mary was by no means his "darling," he had no right whatsoever to expect to hear from her ever again—much less on Christmas Eve—she doubted he cared one bit how she was doing and he knew exactly where she was. It surprised her, at just that moment, how she'd allowed this man to hold such power over her. The time for that was over, and she was ready to end it.

"I'm great actually. Very happy."

"No kidding." Thornton's voice dripped with doubt. "And here I was sure you were calling to ask for your old job back for Christmas. You can have it, you know." His tone implied that he'd be the big man and forgive her the terrible sin of leaving him.

"No thanks, Thornton. I just wanted to call and say Merry Christmas. This will be our last phone conversation. And there will be no more mail. No more communication. I'm done, and I just wanted to tell you myself."

He didn't speak for a moment; Mary heard only the yelling and revelry from wherever he was. People trying too hard to be happy. It sounded so empty.

"Come on now…" he finally said in the fumbling way of someone who can't think of anything better to say.

"No, really. You can tell whoever asks that I wrote the song, but you ought to also tell them that I'm not inclined to give interviews. And if I catch you giving out this number to anyone, I won't be nice about it. I mean it, Thornton."

She heard glasses clinking, as if he'd just taken a swig of a drink. "No, you don't."

"Oh, I do."

Thornton let out a string of the colorful adjectives for which he was famous. Actually, she'd expected to be called far worse—Thornton wasn't at all used to people cutting him off. The language fell sharp and repulsive on her ears. "Be that way," he snapped at the end of the off-color diatribe.

"I'm happy where I am, Thornton. Leave me alone now."

"No problem," he practically shouted in her ear. "You just dropped off the radar, sweetheart."

"I really do wish you a Merry Christmas, Thornton. The Bippo Bear campaign looks like it was everything you wanted it to be. Enjoy your success."

"What's with the holier-than-thou attitude?"

She could just imagine him, pacing the hallway of some posh Chicago bar, tie loosened, drink spilling out of one hand.

"You know what, doll? I'm glad you're gone. Everyone's replaceable. I got people lining up for your job, and none of them will spout sermons at me. You're *gone.*"

With that pronouncement, Thornton hung up on her. And she didn't mind.

She *was* gone. Long gone, and glad of it. Mary wondered, as she hit the disconnect button on her phone, how she'd ever been so afraid of that man. With a flourish, she deleted his contact information from her cell phone. It didn't matter who knew what she'd been, because she knew now who she was. And *Whose* she was.

Emily's shop smelled fabulous when Mary pushed open the door half an hour later. The cinnamon-pine-berry scent of whatever potpourri she had set out—and Emily always had something fragrant and wonderful set out—filled Mary's head with visions of a Dickens Christmas. She could almost imagine a pie baking somewhere behind Emily's counter. Music-box versions of Christmas carols filled the air. Mary placed a small wrapped gift on the counter just as Emily came out from the stock room in the back of her shop. "Oh," Emily said with a bright smile, coming around the counter in a welcoming rush, "it's you. I'm so glad to see you this morning." She wrapped Mary in an enormous hug. "Merry Christmas Eve. How are you? I mean really, after yesterday and all, how are you? I've been sending up prayers for you all night."

"Well, I'm not as bad as I thought. I decided to stay away from the TV news today—if Bippo Bear brawls are breaking out in cities across the country, I'd just as soon not know about it." She could actually joke about Bippo Bears. Mary wasn't sure that day would ever come, much less come on Christmas Eve.

"I think that's a great idea. I'm sure I won't have a free moment to turn one on today, either. I used to stay open late on Christmas Eve, back before Gil." Mary had since learned the long and painful story of Emily and Gil's courtship. It was part of the reason she was here this morning, actually. "Now I close at the regular time—even a bit early this year." She struck a theatrical pose. "I have a performance to prepare for."

Emily's transformation from shy reluctance to a wonderful performance was one of the most rewarding things about Mary's new life in Middleburg. It was so satisfying to watch someone discover a strength or talent. So much more satisfying than even her largest bonus checks at Maxwell Advertising. Mary discovered she could actually thank God for all He'd done in her life this year, even now. She had struggled, no doubt, but the struggles God sent could be trusted as good things. "You'll be great tonight," Mary said to Emily, meaning it. "I know last night was shaky, but I feel good about tonight. So I brought you this." She pointed toward the box. "To say thanks for all your kindness, and decorations, and support, and a little advice I'm about to ask for."

Emily pulled off the wrapping paper to find a box of exotic Chinese tea. "It smells divine." She looked up at Mary with a narrowed eye. "Advice, hm? How about we brew some of this up and have a chat over some tea?"

Mary smiled. "That's exactly what I had in mind."

When the pair had been settled in the little chintz-covered table by Emily's window, and the fragrance of jasmine mixed with the holiday scents around the room, Emily wrapped her hands around her mug and said, "So, what's on your mind?"

"Well," Mary began, "first of all, I wanted to ask you what people think. I know a few people are upset about the Bippo Bear thing, and I understand that, but I don't know how many people are upset with me because I don't think they know me well enough to come to me personally. Yet."

"Are you that worried about what people think?"

"Well, that's just the thing of it. I'm not sure how worried a Christian ought to be about what other people think. I mean look at Mac. He needed to worry, and I'm not sure he did. Should I worry?"

Emily sat back in the little wrought iron chair. "Well, that's a tricky point. One, actually, that Gil has to deal with all the time, especially with all the guys. When you reform young criminals on your farm, you can't ignore what people think, but you can't let it dictate what you do, either. I think the best thing is to ask yourself if what you're doing honors God, and honors what you believe God's will for you is at the time. And you have to be ready for His answers. God likes to shake up our idea of what's a good idea."

"Yeah, I'm coming to understand that part. I thought it was a good idea to hide my former life at first, but I think I would have avoided a lot of problems if I'd told a few people earlier. I needed the Mac Five about a week before I got it, if you ask me."

Emily raised an eyebrow. "The 'Mac Five'?"

"Mac's trademark crisis management plan. Sort of a 'pick five people you can trust and let them help you solve the problem' thing. Involving circles and diagrams and all that engineering stuff Mac loves. You were in my Mac Five, by the way, I just never got around to talking to anyone but Mac and Pastor Dave before it all…well, you know."

"Oh, boy, do I know." She gave Mary an inquisitive look. "But why do I think I don't know all of it?"

Dinah had talked about Emily's canny intuition. It seemed like Middleburg was filled with women who knew what anyone *really* wanted to talk about before they could get the words out of their mouths. "Well, I wanted to ask you, actually, about Gil. About you and Gil."

Emily smiled. "No, you didn't. You wanted to ask me

if it's okay to fall for someone like Mac even though he hurt you."

Mary tried not to knock over her tea. It was a full minute of choking before she could say, "Wow, you're good."

"No, just observant. You two couldn't take your eyes off each other at the party. And he talks about you a lot. And I could see how miserable you both were last night. And, yes, I have a little experience with a wounded heart." The tender way Emily put a hand on Mary's arm, Mary thought her feelings of shock and exposure must be flooding her face.

"I don't know what to do," Mary admitted finally, surprised to find tears gathering behind her eyes. "I don't know what to feel or think. I shouldn't care for him. Not now, not so soon. The timing's all wrong."

"Maybe only to you," Emily replied. "The two of you have been through a lot in a short time, it's true. But sometimes that's just God's way of getting our attention."

Mary watched the steam from the tea make graceful curves in the air. "I forgave him last night. I didn't think I had it in me, but when he explained how he felt, it was like I suddenly had the ability to do it when I never thought I would. And it was both very hard and not hard at all, which makes no sense."

"It makes a whole lot of sense to me," Emily asserted. "That's what faith does. It gives us the ability to do things that should feel impossible. Mercy is always undeserved. It can never be earned, only given." Her smile was warm and understanding. "I'm a big believer in mercy. It took me a while to get there, but that's a story for another time. Do you think there's something worthwhile between you and Mac?"

"I do." Mary couldn't believe a tear was finding its way

down her cheek. This all seemed to be ridiculously melo-dramatic, but she couldn't seem to stop the flood of emotions. "I know it's crazy, but I do."

"Then you should know I had a particular customer this morning. A man—oh, I'd say just a few days shy of thirty—looking for the perfect gift for someone. He drove an orange sports car, by the way. He wanted a star for the top of a young lady's tree. The absolute best star I had, because he said they had a history of trouble with stars, and that he had a lot to make up to her, but that she meant a lot to him." Emily smiled. "You have any idea who that might be?"

Mary's pulse started racing. She'd noticed Mac wasn't in the office this morning. Mary felt something electric run down her spine. A giddy energy that made her unable to hide the blushing grin she felt break out on her face. "Mac was here?"

"Good thing you've got it for that man something fierce, because from where I sit, he's got it something fierce for you. Go on home. We can finish our tea another time, and I believe you have someone waiting for you there."

I could be sitting at my desk. I could be getting work done. Well, I could be pretending to get work done. Mac sat on the steps leading up to Mary's apartment and fiddled with the yellow gift bag from Emily's shop. He'd once kidded Gil for holding one of those bags—Emily always stuffed her bags so full of frilly tissue that no man could hold his head upright while carrying the thing. Gil's face had looked exactly like he now felt. Ridiculous but unable to help himself.

It can wait.

No, it can't.

He had to know things were set right between himself and Mary. He had to declare his…his what? He didn't really know. He mostly just had to know if she felt what he felt. If that thing that wouldn't let him alone—the thing that wouldn't let him think or sleep and drove him to do things like 'fess up decades-old secrets—if that thing wouldn't let her alone, either. He'd seen it, well, glimpses of it for weeks and even last night in spite of all the pain. What was that old saying about "you only hurt the ones you love?"

Did he love her? Maybe. She sure affected him as no other woman ever did. She was beautiful—she'd practically knocked the breath out of him when she came down the stairs in that soft green sweater for Gil's Christmas party—but it was more than that. He'd always been an ambitious man, but Mary somehow pulled inner aspirations out of him. Urges to be a different *kind* of man, to reach for a different, deeper faith. Mostly he knew that if she ever looked at him again with the hurt and betrayal she had yesterday afternoon in his office, he wouldn't live through it. And so he was willing to do anything and everything— including sitting on some steps bearing a frilly yellow bag—to win her favor.

Oh, Jesus, I won't last another half hour. Have mercy on me, I'm dying here. Mac tunneled one hand through his hair and pushed out a breath. *If it's all going to go sour, just get it over with. But please, please don't let it go sour. I don't know how You did all this, but I'm willing to see it through to the end if You'll just cut me a little slack here.*

He looked up and saw Mary through the window in the door at the bottom of the stairway. She was standing in the foyer that joined her door, his office door, and Dinah's bakery; peering into his office window. Looking for him.

Oh, Lord, please let her be looking for me and not looking to avoid me.

She stepped to the door and fumbled for her keys, and Mac felt his blood go still. He'd know the second she looked at him. It would all be there in her eyes—it was always there in her eyes—and he'd know if he stood any chance at all. He'd never deserved mercy less or craved it more.

She looked up, held his eyes for a moment that seemed to last all day, and let a tender smile steal across her face. She pushed open the door and stood at the bottom of the stairs, gazing up at him. She was, at that moment, the most welcome sight in all of history. She tucked a strand of hair behind her ear, and feelings scattered across his chest like shock waves. "Hi," she said softly, putting one foot on the first step.

"Are you okay this morning?" He felt as inelegant as a sixth grade boy, about to break out in sweat any minute.

"Yeah, actually I am. I think it's going to be okay tonight. How'd it go with Howard?"

Mac swallowed. "Harder than I thought, but better than I thought. He made no bones about agreeing I should pull out of the race. I wouldn't exactly call him gracious. He could have put it better than 'you've got some growing up to do.'"

Mary came up a step. "Even I know Howard doesn't do subtle. To him, you're still in your twenties, which means you're a young'un. Just a smart-aleck kid."

"'Young'un'? Aren't you from Chicago? Besides, I like to think I'm becoming a wise man."

"No, the wise men don't show up until scene four tonight. But you do have a history of seeking stars, so there's hope for you yet."

Taking a deep breath, Mac held up the bag. "Merry Christmas," he said, his voice feeling foreign in his own throat. "It's not a bear, I promise." He realized, with an absurd relief, that she was as flustered as he was. He chose to believe that meant he stood a chance. "I'm coming tonight."

"Breaking with MacCarthy tradition?" Her smile broadened and she came up more steps.

Time to go for broke. "Because you asked me to." He saw her pull in a breath. She was two steps below him, her face even with him as he sat on the pair of steps above her. He thought if he stood up now, the way the oxygen seemed to be thinning right out of the room, he'd fall clean down the stairs in a stunned heap of nerves. He placed the bag in her hands. "I need you to have this."

She blushed, then pulled at the tissue paper until it revealed the spun glass star with silver and gold strands spiraling around each other in the glass. It was an exquisite, exorbitant piece of artwork, a stunning sculpture, and he'd have gladly paid three times what Emily charged him just to put it in Mary's hands this morning. They'd shared that first moment of secrets in the steeple beside the broken star. She'd forgiven him under the big star in the sanctuary. He wanted to—*had* to be the one to give her a star for her tree today, Christmas Eve.

"Oh, Mac, it's beautiful." She ran her hand across the delicate angles and Mac felt it down the back of his neck. "You didn't have to…."

"Yes," he interrupted, "I did. I…I need to know we can get past all this. I need to know I haven't thrown away what…" the rest of the words tangled up in his throat.

"You want to help me get this on top of the tree?"

Her voice was warm and soft and charmingly nervous. He hadn't lost his chance with her. The realization sent relief pouring through him.

"More than anything." That sounded dorky, but he was past caring.

She let him into her apartment, the morning sun streaming through the big front windows. It was a blue-skied Kentucky winter's day, and her bedecked tree shimmered in the splashes of sunlight. It was a huge tree—probably twice the size she'd have chosen for herself—and he'd nearly thrown his back out getting that behemoth up her stairs and through her front door. Still, he was glad to notice there was still a foot or two between the top of the tree and her apartment's high ceilings. "You'll need a chair to get up there," he remarked, walking into the kitchen. He carried a kitchen chair into the living room and planted it next to the tree while she put down the bag and slipped the final tags off the star.

"I wasn't sure there'd be room," she joked as she brought the star over to the tree.

Mac held out his hand to help her up onto the chair. It felt small and perfect in his palm, and he was sure she sucked her breath in the way he did when they touched. With one hand holding hers and the other gripping the chair to keep her safe, he helped her step up. Then, to his reluctant joy, he found it necessary to hold her waist while she used both hands to settle the star on top of the tree. So much for his original intentions to keep a restrained distance from her.

"Oops…wait a minute…there, I got it. Yep, it just fits." She made a delightful sighing sound. "Oh, Mac, it's perfect."

She turned in the chair so that Mac was holding her

waist as she stood above him, and it struck him again how absolutely beautiful she was. She placed her hands on his shoulders, and any shreds of control he had left evaporated into the sunlight that gilt her hair. He hoisted her down from the chair and stood dumbstruck by the color of her eyes. "I'm so glad," he said in a wobbly voice that didn't even seem to belong to him.

After a moment—or maybe it was an hour, he couldn't be sure—she lay her fingers against his jaw. Her face bore a pleased but puzzled expression, as if she was trying to work out a very happy riddle.

"How'd we get here?"

Even though it was a vague question, he knew exactly what she meant. He'd asked it of himself—of God—repeatedly over the last day. How had they managed this rocky path to the brink of such an implausible relationship? "I reckon that's one of the things God does best," he said, settling his hands around her, astounded by how perfectly she fit in his arms. "He knows what we need better than we do, and just how to get us to sit up and take notice. I'm pretty sure I'd have never figured this out on my own."

She let her full hand settle against his jaw. "It's harder than I thought. But it's better than I thought, too."

"Ain't it?" Mac couldn't stand it anymore. He leaned down and kissed her. Carefully, tenderly at first, until she brought both arms up to circle his neck and shot his restraint to pieces. They kissed with surprise and wonder and freedom until Mac pulled away, nearly gasping from the power of it. "*That* was better than I thought. And I thought about that way too much."

Mary laughed and settled herself into the perfect spot under his chin. Mac let his head touch her hair and decided the world had achieved perfection. Middleburg's first-ever Christmas Eve Drama and Potluck could implode to ashes and he'd still call this the Best Christmas Ever.

"Dave was right," Mary said as she twisted her head up to meet his gaze.

"Pastor Dave? How so?"

"He said that even when it looks awful, you can count on God's plan because His end is always better than anything we could dream up for ourselves."

"Yep," Mac agreed, kissing the top of her forehead just because it felt so wonderful to do so. "I think Dave's right on the money." He kissed another perfect spot, this one above her right eye. "Merry Christmas, Mary Thorpe."

"Merry Christmas…hey, your first name's Joe, isn't it?"

Mac applied a teasingly sour face. "We try not to mention that around these parts."

She snuggled against him with a sigh he felt to the soles of his feet. "Mary and Joseph. It's just too funny."

"No it's not. It's absurd."

"This from the man with the operatic cockatoo."

Mac let out a breath. He'd forgotten all about that. "Yeah, about Curly…"

"Oh, no," Mary said, "I really like him, I was just kidding you."

Mac pulled away. "No, I mean there's something about Curly." In the intensity of the morning, Mac hadn't yet had the chance to bring up his current dilemma. "I learned something about Curly while I was gone last night."

"What?"

Mac picked up the chair and returned it to the kitchen table. "It seems my feathered friend doesn't care for your little blue buddies. I left my nephew's Bippo Bear out on the dining room table while we were at rehearsal last night so I could wrap it this morning, and well, Curly had at it." He threw his hands up in the air. "That mangy bird shredded it. I came home to a very expensive fuzzy blue blizzard."

Mary gasped, wide-eyed. "Curly ate your Bippo Bear?"

"Not exactly. He just demolished it. I found one ear on top of my refrigerator and an eye in my bathtub. The only way I can give Robby his Bippo Bear now is in a plastic bag. I'm done for."

"Good thing you know someone on the inside," she smiled. Now it was her turn to pretend at annoyance. "I happen to have a spare Bippo Bear or two in my own personal collection. I've kept them hidden in the bottom of my closet. But it'll cost you something fierce."

"You have no idea how much I was hoping you'd say that. Name your price. I'm prepared to pay anything."

Those creamy arms wrapped around his neck again, and Mac thought there wasn't a single thing she couldn't ask of him. "A potluck dish, one perfect performance and maybe a few more of those kisses."

Mac leaned in, delighted to oblige. "Wow. Best bargain ever."

Chapter Eighteen

It was after midnight, and very few people showed any signs of wanting to leave the MCC basement where the Christmas Eve potluck was still going in full swing. As a matter of fact, cries of "Merry Christmas" rung out at midnight, and only those with young children had gone home. Everyone else stayed eating and chatting and singing every verse of every Christmas carol until voices were hoarse. The whole evening had the happy charm of an old Bing Crosby movie, and Mary soaked in every minute of it as if life had started all over again this morning. Then again, perhaps it had. Was everyone's first Christmas as a new believer like this? Or had she been given some special gift?

Pastor Dave came up and gave her a big hug. "Howard asked me this morning if I regretted hiring you. I told him 'not one bit' then, and I feel doubly glad now. Well done, Mary. Well done."

"Thanks," she responded and hugged him right back. "For everything."

"You know," Pastor Dave said as he saw Howard

making his way across the room toward Mary, "I think you succeeded on all fronts. We may have taken the long road to unity, but I have a feeling we got there all the same. Course there's really only one man who can tell you if that's true…." The pastor stepped back to allow Howard his say. He didn't look as cheery as some of the other guests, but he didn't look ready to run her out of town, either.

"I'm not known for keeping my opinions to myself, Miss Thorpe," he began. "And I still wish you'd have been upfront about your résumé."

"I think I agree with you, Howard, for what it's worth. It was a mistake not to bring it up."

"Speaking of mistakes, you'll be surprised to know I don't mind them much." He tucked his hands in his pockets and rocked back on his heels. "Mistakes are life's best teachers, if you ask me. It's folks who don't own up to their mistakes that get under my skin. But I reckon you already knew that."

It wasn't hard to know what got under Howard's skin. He made no efforts to hide it, ever. "I figured it out pretty quick."

"So I'm going to own up to mine and say you did a good job here. This potluck thing was a good idea, and I was wrong about it at first."

He was going out of his way to say she'd done well, and that made her feel good. "Thanks for the vote of confidence, Howard. It means a lot."

"Ah, yes, votes," Howard said with an odd tone of voice. "Tricky things."

"Mac pulling out of the race pretty much hands you another term as mayor, doesn't it?"

"It does." His comment was carefully neutral, but not

all together comfortable. "Unfortunate business, all of it. I actually think MacCarthy has promise." He smiled and offered her a cookie from the table they were standing near—one of Dinah's gingerbread menagerie. "He was running for *half* the right reasons." He raised a suspicious eyebrow at Dinah's gingerbread hippopotamus before taking a healthy bite. "Besides," he went on, "that fellow had better find a longer fuse to his temper if he's going to last ten minutes in my shoes."

Mary stared across the room where Mac was having a warm conversation with his parents. It had been a tough evening—not everyone was ready to give Mac a second chance, or quick to forgive him for his youthful faults. The room still contained its fair share of cold shoulders, despite the holiday glow. "Mac says he's still sure God wanted him to run, but now it wasn't to be mayor, it was to learn a lesson."

"And do you think he has?" Howard asked, following her stare and giving out a sigh. "Learned the lesson, that is?"

"I do." She gave Howard a grin. "He may actually be less trouble to you now." She pointed at the last bit of yuletide hippo as Howard popped it into his mouth. "Maybe we should talk Dinah into running for mayor. *She* still loves to give you the business."

"Young lady, that is an absolutely hideous idea. Keep it to yourself." His speech was dark and formal, but his eyes twinkled. "Merry Christmas, Mary."

"Merry Christmas, Howard."

Epilogue

Mary was staring into the roaring fire at the MacCarthy house when Mac caught her by the elbow from behind. "Come here, quick," he whispered. "You need to see this."

Mac's parents' house was brimming with MacCarthys of all shapes and sizes, from infants to grandparents. From the moment they'd arrived, the house was bursting with enough noise and chaos that Mary could understand Mac's need for peace and quiet before weathering this familial storm.

"What?" she asked, only to be "shushed" by Mac as he led her through the house down to what Mrs. MacCarthy called "the rumpus room," which was basically a finished den currently overrun with grandchildren.

Grandchildren who were singing.

As Mac and Mary hid at the top of the stairs, Mary saw a gaggle of children gathered around Mac's nephew, many of them reaching out to touch the Bippo Bear she'd supplied. Uncle Mac had indeed "come through" with the gotta-have Bippo Bear by raiding Mary's private stash. As such, Robby was the envy of his peers. As they stroked and pawed and fussed with the bear, tiny voices broke out repeatedly in the jingle. *Her* jingle. Only it wasn't that whining, pleading version the news stories ran or the sugary, chirpy version on the commercial. It was sweet children's voices singing out of sheer Christmas happiness. She'd never heard anything like it in her life. Mary felt like her heart had, as Dr. Seuss so aptly put it, "grown three sizes that day."

"Wow."

"Yeah," said Mac softly into her ear. "I thought you needed to see this. You did this."

She looked back at him, affection for him flooding her triple-sized heart. "I did, didn't I?" She listened for another wondrous moment. "I've never heard kids singing it before. I mean really singing it, not whining it."

Mac looked at her. "You weren't there when they had the kids singing it for the commercial?"

She laughed. "Oh, Mac, kids don't sing on commercials. We hire actors who can sound like kids." She remembered the days when things like that sounded perfectly normal to her.

Mac's expression told her it sounded ridiculous to him. "You gotta be kidding me."

"No," she said, allowing herself the delightful luxury of setting into this arms as they slipped around her waist. "It's true."

"I'll never trust another television commercial as long as I live," he teased into the back of her neck, making tingles run down her spine. "Now I know the ugly truth about you ad people."

"We're not all bad. Just some. Same as people who do anything for a living. Like engineers. Or mayors."

"Or former mayoral candidates/engineers?"

"No," Mary objected. "Those are looking pretty good right now." She reached up and let one hand wander through his sandy hair. His eyes fell shut and his head swayed involuntarily toward her touch.

"When are we going to let people know?" Mac asked.

"When I'm ready, and not a moment before. Got that?" Mary gave him as serious a look as she could manage under the circumstances. There would be no more breaches of confidence between them. She was strong enough to demand that now. She also was pretty sure she wouldn't be able to hold it in for long. "Like when you're thirty."

Mac rolled his eyes and groaned. "I'll never last five days." The playfulness left his eyes, replaced by a promise that he'd never betray her again. "But I'll find a way." Mac's voice was low and alluring. "How about five *minutes?* I'm an impatient guy."

She laughed softly, enjoying the sway she held over him. And that it didn't feel anything like manipulation. It felt more like a gift from God. "Maybe four. You know us advertising types. We're always open to negotiation." She leaned in and gave him a gentle kiss in the shadowed privacy of the den stairway, serenaded by the Bippo Bear song, which had just become her favorite piece of music, ever.

* * * * *

Dear Reader,

I've gotten sucked up in the Christmas "gotta have" machine as much as any living human being. I love celebrations, even if the preparation can rob me of every shred of peace I once had. We've all had wonderful Christmases, and holidays we'd just as soon forget. This side of heaven, we're going to muck it all up on a regular basis. As Pastor Dave puts it, it's why Christ came in the first place. And the first place in all our Christmases should always be the Christ child whose coming we celebrate. Some deep part of us knows that when we get that focus right, the rest will fall into place. If only we'd tune out all the hubbub and *listen* to that deep part. I hope this story helps you to seek a deep and meaningful Christmas, no matter how the details spin around you. I would love to hear from you at alliepleiter.com or P.O. Box 7026, Villa Park, IL 60181.

Blessed Christmas to you all!

Allie Pleiter

QUESTIONS FOR DISCUSSION

1. What's been your "Bippo Bear"? Did you have a time when you went crazy over a particular gift for someone? Did you regret it later?

2. Would you have run against Howard? Why or why not?

3. Is there something about your current life that "chafes" at you the way Mary's job did? What can you do about it?

4. Mary chose a drastic option in moving away from her home and job. Would you have done the same? Why or why not?

5. What do you think *really* drove Mac to run for mayor?

6. If you sat on MCC's council, would you have voted for mounting the Christmas drama? Do you think it was a good solution to Middleburg's "mayoral malaise"?

7. Emily channeled her anxiety about being pregnant into holiday decorating. Have you had an experience like that in coping with a stressful situation? Did it work? Or did it cause more problems?

8. Could Middleburg have avoided this whole conflict? How?

9. Is Mac right or wrong to resist a relationship with a fellow Christian who he feels is in "a different place" than him spiritually?

10. What—emotionally and spiritually—has it cost Mac to keep his secret? Would he be a different man now if he had come forward when he was younger?

11. Have you ever had a secret you felt would change the way people viewed you? What's the risk—spiritually and emotionally—in revealing it? What might you gain?

12. Why are we so easily drawn into the holiday frenzy? Are there things you can do to keep your focus in the right place? Pick one of your ideas to implement this Christmas season.

13. Mary receives many acts of kindness from Middleburg residents. What act of kindness can you do to brighten someone's holiday season?

When a young Roman woman is wrenched from the safety of her family and sold into slavery, she finds herself at the mercy of the most famous gladiator in Rome. In God's plan, a master and his slave just might fall in love....

Turn the page for a sneak preview of
THE GLADIATOR
by Carla Capshaw
Available in November 2009
from Love Inspired® Historical

Rome, 81 A.D.

Angry, unfamiliar voices penetrated Pelonia's awareness. Floating between wakefulness and dark, she couldn't budge. Every muscle ached. A sharp pain drummed against her skull.

The voices died away, then a woman's words broke through the haze.

"My name is Lucia. Can you hear me?" The woman pressed a cup of water to Pelonia's cracked lips. "What shall I call you?"

Pelonia coughed as the cool liquid trickled down her arid throat. "Pel...Pelonia."

"Do you remember what happened to you? You were struck on the head and injured. I've been giving you opium to soothe you, but you're far from recovered."

Her eyelids too heavy to open, Pelonia licked her chapped lips.

Gradually her mind began to make sense of her surroundings. The warmth must be sunshine, because the scent of wood smoke hung in the air. Her pallet was a coarse woolen blanket on the hard ground. Dirt clung to her skin and each of her sore muscles longed for the softness of her bed at home.

Home.

Where was she if not in the comfort of her father's Umbrian villa? Who was this woman Lucia? She couldn't remember.

Icy fingers of fear gripped her heart as one by one her memories returned. First the attack, then her father's murder. Raw grief squeezed her chest.

Confusion surrounded her. Where was her uncle? She remembered the slave caravan, his threat to sell her, but nothing more.

Panic forced her eyes open. She managed to focus on the young woman's face above her.

"The master will be here soon." A smile tilted Lucia's thin lips, but didn't touch her honey-brown eyes.

"Where…am I?" she asked, the words grating in her throat.

"You're in the home of Caros Viriathos."

The name meant nothing to Pelonia. She prayed God had delivered her into the hands of a kind man, someone who would help her contact her cousin Tiberia.

Her eyes closed with fatigue. "How…how long have I…been here?"

"Four days and this morning. You've been in and out of sleep. I'll order you a bowl of broth. You should eat to bolster your strength."

Four days, and she remembered nothing. Tiberia must be frantic wondering why she'd failed to attend her wedding.

She opened her eyes. "I must—"

"Don't speak. Now that you've woken, Gaius, our master's steward, says you have one week to recover. Then your labor begins."

"My cousin. I must…"

"You're a slave in the Ludus Maximus now. A possession of the *lanista,* Caros Viriathos."

Lanista? A vile *gladiator* trainer?

"No!"

Lucia crossed her arms over her buxom chest. "We will see."

Heavy footsteps crunched on the rushes strewn across the floor. The new arrival stopped out of Pelonia's view.

The nauseating ache in her head increased without mercy. What had she done to make God despise her?

Focusing on Lucia, she saw the young woman's face light with pleasure.

"Master," Lucia greeted, jumping to her feet. "The new slave is finally awake. She calls herself Pelonia. She's weak and the medicine I gave her has run its course."

"Then give her more if she needs it."

The man's deep voice poured over Pelonia like the soothing water of a bath. She turned her head, ignoring the jab of pain that pierced her skull.

"You mustn't move your head," Lucia snapped, "or you might injure yourself further."

Pelonia stiffened. She wasn't accustomed to taking orders from slaves.

Lucia glanced toward the door. "She's argumentative. I have a hunch she'll be difficult. She denies she's your slave."

Silence followed Lucia's remark. Would this man who claimed to own her kill or beat her? Was he a cruel barbarian?

She sensed him move closer. Her tension rose as if she were prey in the sights of a hungry lion. At last the lion crossed to where she could see him.

Sunlight streaming through the window enveloped the giant, giving his dark hair a golden glow. A crisp, light-colored tunic draped across his shoulders and chest contrasted sharply with the rich copper of his skin. Gold bands around his upper arms emphasized the thickness of his muscles, the physical power he held in check.

Her breath hitched in her throat. She could only stare. Without a doubt, the man could crush her if he chose.

"So, you are called Pelonia," he said. "And my healer believes you wish to fight me."

Her gaze locked with the unusual blue of his forceful glare. For the first time she understood how the Hebrew, David, must have suffered when he faced Goliath. Swallowing the lump of fear in her throat, she nodded. "If I must."

"If you must?" Caros eyed Pelonia with a mix of irritation and respect. With her tunic filthy and torn, her dark hair in disarray and her bruises healing, his new slave looked like a wounded goddess. But she was just an ordinary woman. Why did she think she could defy him?

"Then let the games begin," he said, his voice thick with mockery.

"You think…this…this is a game?" she asked faintly.

The roughness of her voice reminded him of her body's weakened condition—a frailty her spirit clearly didn't share. Crouching beside her, he ran his forefinger over the yellowed bruise on her cheek. She closed her eyes and sighed as though his touch somehow soothed her.

Her guileless response unnerved him. The need to protect her enveloped him, a sensation he hadn't known since the deaths of his mother and sisters. As a slave, he'd been beaten on many occasions in an effort to conquer his will. That no one ever succeeded was a matter of pride for him. Much to his surprise, he had no wish to see this girl broken either.

"Of course it's a game. And I will be the victor."

Defiance flamed in the depths of her large, doe-brown eyes. She didn't speak and he admired her restraint when he could see she wanted to flay him.

"You might as well give in now, my prize. I own you whether you will it or not."

He gripped her chin and forced her to look at him.

"Admit it," he said. "Then you can return to your sleep."

She shook her head. "No. No one owns me...no one but my God."

"And who might your god be? Jupiter? Apollo? Or maybe you worship the god of the sea. Do you think Neptune will rescue you?"

"The Christ."

Caros wondered if she were a fool or had a wish for death. "Say that to the wrong person, Pelonia, and you'll find yourself facing the lions."

"I already am."

He laughed. "So you think of me as a ferocious beast?"

Her silence amused him all the more. "Good. It suits me well to know you realize I'm untamed and capable of tearing you limb from limb."

"Then do your worst. Death is better...than being owned."

Caros suddenly noticed Pelonia had grown pale and weaker still.

He berated himself for depleting her meager strength when he should have been encouraging her to heal. He lifted her into his arms.

She weighed no more than a laurel leaf. Had he pushed her to the brink of death?

Holding her tight against his chest, he whispered near her ear. "Tell me, *mea carissima*. What can I do to aid you? What can I do to ease your plight?"

"Find…Tiberia," she whispered, the dregs of her strength draining away. "And free me."

* * * * *

Will Pelonia ever convince Caros of who she is and where she truly belongs? Or will their growing love bind her to him for all time?

Find out in
THE GLADIATOR
by Carla Capshaw
Available in November 2009
from Love Inspired® Historical

REQUEST YOUR FREE BOOKS!

2 FREE INSPIRATIONAL NOVELS
PLUS 2
FREE
MYSTERY GIFTS

YES! Please send me 2 FREE Love Inspired® novels and my 2 FREE mystery gifts (gifts are worth about $10). After receiving them, if I don't wish to receive any more books, I can return the shipping statement marked "cancel". If I don't cancel, I will receive 4 brand-new novels every month and be billed just $4.24 per book in the U.S. or $4.74 per book in Canada. That's a savings of over 20% off the cover price. It's quite a bargain! Shipping and handling is just 50¢ per book.* I understand that accepting the 2 free books and gifts places me under no obligation to buy anything. I can always return a shipment and cancel at any time. Even if I never buy another book, the two free books and gifts are mine to keep forever.

113 IDN EYK2 313 IDN EYLE

Name	(PLEASE PRINT)	
Address		Apt. #
City	State/Prov.	Zip/Postal Code

Signature (if under 18, a parent or guardian must sign)

Mail to Steeple Hill Reader Service:
IN U.S.A.: P.O. Box 1867, Buffalo, NY 14240-1867
IN CANADA: P.O. Box 609, Fort Erie, Ontario L2A 5X3

Not valid to current subscribers of Love Inspired books.

Want to try two free books from another series?
Call 1-800-873-8635 or visit www.morefreebooks.com

* Terms and prices subject to change without notice. Prices do not include applicable taxes. Sales tax applicable in N.Y. Canadian residents will be charged applicable provincial taxes and GST. Offer not valid in Quebec. This offer is limited to one order per household. All orders subject to approval. Credit or debit balances in a customer's account(s) may be offset by any other outstanding balance owed by or to the customer. Please allow 4 to 6 weeks for delivery. Offer available while quantities last.

Your Privacy: Steeple Hill Books is committed to protecting your privacy. Our Privacy Policy is available online at www.SteepleHill.com or upon request from the Reader Service. From time to time we make our lists of customers available to reputable third parties who may have a product or service of interest to you. If you would prefer we not share your name and address, please check here. ☐

LIREG09

Love Inspired

TITLES AVAILABLE NEXT MONTH
Available October 27, 2009

TOGETHER FOR THE HOLIDAYS by Margaret Daley
Fostered by Love

Single mother Lisa Morgan only wants to raise her son with love and good values. Yet when a world-weary cop becomes the boy's reluctant father figure, Lisa discovers she has a Christmas wish as well....

A FAMILY FOR THANKSGIVING by Patricia Davids
After the Storm

Nicki Appleton may have to say goodbye to the sweet toddler she took in after the tornado. Yet when the man she once loved comes home to High Plains, can she count on Clay Logan to be her family for Thanksgiving—and forever?

CLOSE TO HOME by Carolyne Aarsen

Jace Scholte was the town bad boy—until he fell for Dodie Westerveld. But instead of marrying him, Dodie ran away without a word. Now, they're both back in town. But Dodie still won't talk about the past....

BLESSINGS OF THE SEASON by Annie Jones and Brenda Minton

Two heartwarming holiday stories.

In "The Holiday Husband," Addie McCoy's holidays have never been traditional. Could Nate Browder be the perfect old-fashioned husband? In "The Christmas Letter," single mom Isabella Grant's dreams of family come true when a handsome soldier comes knocking on her door!

HIS COWGIRL BRIDE by Debra Clopton

Former bronc rider Brent Stockwell doesn't think *ladies* belong in the pen or his life. But cowgirl Tacy Jones has come to Mule Hollow to train wild horses and she's determined to change his mind—and his heart.

A FOREVER CHRISTMAS by Missy Tippens

Busy single dad Gregory Jones doesn't have much time to spend with his sons. When Sarah Radcliffe tries to teach him that love and attention are the greatest Christmas gifts of all, will he realize his love is the perfect gift for Sarah as well?

LICNMBPA1009